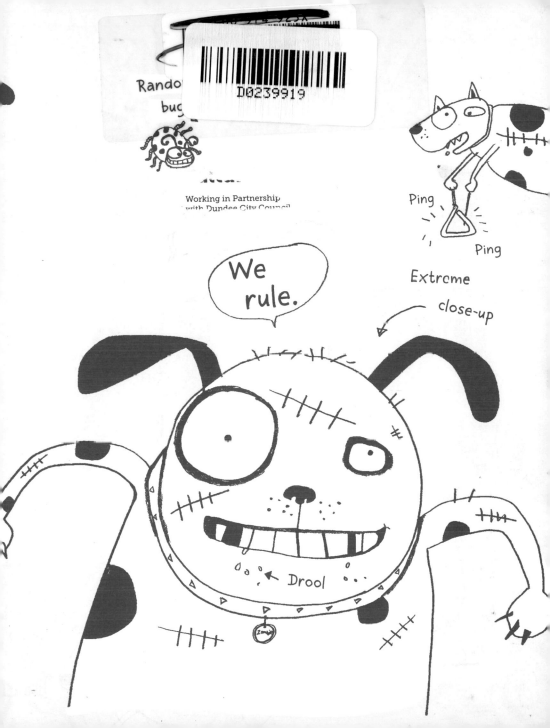

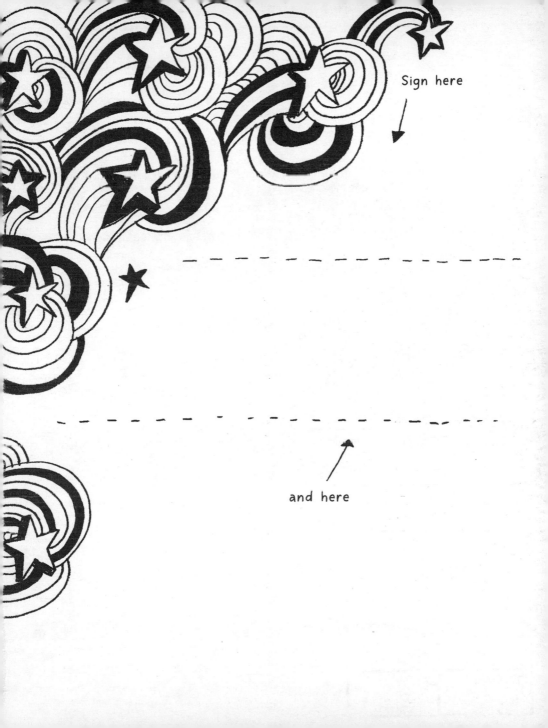

Sign here

and here

Scholastic Children's Books
An imprint of Scholastic Ltd
Euston House, 24 Eversholt Street, London, NW1 1DB, UK
Registered office: Westfield Road, Southam, Warwickshire, CV47 0RA
SCHOLASTIC and associated logos are trademarks and/or
registered trademarks of Scholastic Inc.

First published in the UK by Scholastic Ltd, 2016

Copyright © Liz Pichon Ltd, 2016

The right of Liz Pichon to be identified as the author and illustrator of this
work has been asserted by her.

ISBN 978 1407 17134 0

A CIP catalogue record for this book
is available from the British Library.

Printed by CPI Group (UK) Ltd, Croydon, CR0 4YY
Papers used by Scholastic Children's Books are made
from wood grown in sustainable forests.

5 7 9 10 8 6

This is a work of fiction. Names, characters, places, incidents
and dialogues are products of the author's imagination or are used
fictitiously. Any resemblance to actual people, living or dead,
events or locales is entirely coincidental.

www.scholastic.co.uk

Hangry*
DogZombi*

*Hungry and Angry

DogZombies RuLE
(for now)

by Liz Pichon

Another Hangry Dogzombie →

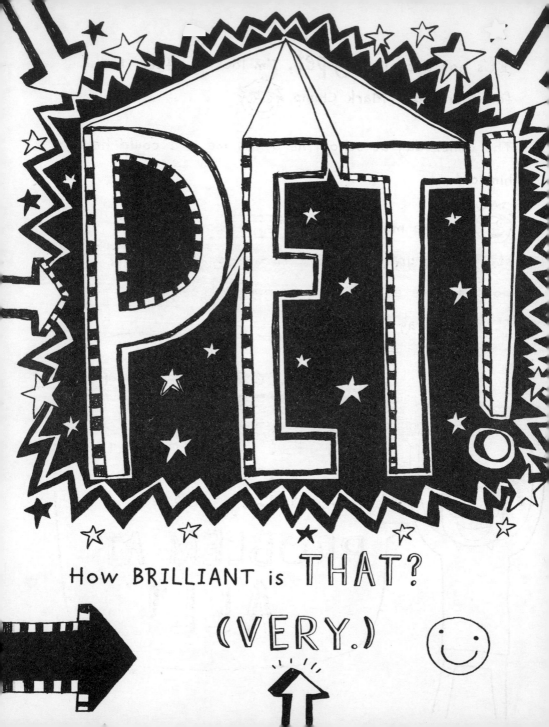

It's not actually **my pet**, I'm looking after it for a friend – Mark Clump.

The other day at school he asked me if I could help him out.

"We're moving house so I have to stay at my granny's for a few days. But she doesn't have enough room for ALL my **pets**. Straight away I shouted,

YES! I CAN HELP! I'll LOOK AFTER YOUR PET, NO PROBLEM AT ALL!

I was SO KEEN that I didn't even ask him WHICH **pet** he was talking about. Mark has a LOT of **pets**. Some of them would be easier to look after than others.

"THANKS, Tom! I'll come over to yours after school and bring EVERYTHING with me, if that's OK?"

"GREAT," I told him.

It was only as I walked back to class that I started to think...

On a scale of 1 ⟹ to 10: how HAPPY would Mum and Dad be about me looking after a *pet?*

😠 Furious			🙁 Not happy			🙂 Happy		😁 Delighted	
1	2	3	4	5	6	7	8	9	10

On a scale of 1 to 10: how happy would Delia be about me keeping a *pet.*

About here

😠 Furious			🙁 Not happy			🙂 Happy		😁 Delighted	
1	2	3	4	5	6	7	8	9	10

This is because Delia is **allergic** to some **pets.** She's allergic to other things too, like

FUN

(It's true. My sister is a **weirdo**.)

I knew it wasn't going to be easy convincing Mum and Dad about the **pet** but I had to **TRY** because I was really looking forward to it now. (Here's my "**EXCITED** about a **pet**" face.)

When I sat down at my desk, Marcus Meldrew looked me up and down. "Why are **YOU** smiling so much? Have you forgotten we've got MATHS this afternoon?"

(I had.)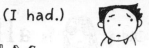

STUPIDLY, I only went and told him

about Mark's **pet.**

"I'm looking after it for him while he's at his granny's. That's why I'm in a good mood."

"You're looking after Mark's **pet** SNAKE?"

"**N**o, not his SNAKE. One of his OTHER **pets,**" I said confidently.

(I'd forgotten about his Snake.)

"I bet it IS his snake. Do you want to know why?"

"Not really," I sighed.

He ignored me and carried on talking.

"Mark's granny will **NOT** want a SNAKE in her house because it might ESCAPE and try to **EAT** her."

Yum.

7

At this point **AMY** stopped reading her book and said,

"For your information, Mark has a corn snake and corn snakes DON'T eat people."

"SEE! **AMY** knows. I'm **not** looking after his snake anyway,"

Hic.

I told Marcus, hoping he'd stop interfering. He didn't.

"There's a FIRST time for everything, Tom. Once that snake's in YOUR house, he could wake up really hungry, slither towards you, then

CHOMP! You're GONE, or at least CHEWED." Marcus was pretending his arm was a snake now.

Slurp

WHY did I tell him anything? I should have just kept quiet.

He carried on doing his silly snake impression until his arm got tired.

Then he HISSSSSSSSSSSSed at me instead ...

HISSSSSSSSSSSS!

Ow!

... which was annoying.

AMY looked up again.

"Put a sock in it, Marcus. I'm trying to read."

"EXACTLY. Shhhhhh, will you?" I agreed.

"I thought your sister was allergic to animals?" AMY suddenly asked me.

(As well as being SUPER smart she also has a very good memory.)

"**Yes,** she is. BUT I have an **EXCELLENT PLAN** to get around that problem," I explained while trying to look thoughtful and clever at the same time.

Clever

Thoughtful

SIGH  "I bet you do..." **AMY** said quietly, and she carried on reading.

(I didn't have a plan – not **YET** anyway.)
It was during **Mr Fullerman's** unbelievably **L O N G** maths lesson that my PLAN came together.

If Mum and Dad said **NO** to me keeping a **pet,** then smuggling it into the house might work. Or keeping it in the garden.
I drew out a few different ideas for different **pets...**

... while expertly keeping my "I'm doing MATHS"
face on the whole time.
Which wasn't easy to do.

Maths grimace

My expression worked right up until Marcus started

L O O K I N G over my shoulder

and hisssssssssssssssssing at me AGAIN.

(Groan.)

Hissssssssss

"Shhhhhhhh," I told him,
trying not to bring attention to myself.

"What kind of MATHS is that?"

Marcus said, not leaving me alone at all.

STRAIGHT AWAY

Mr Fullerman looked in our direction.

"You two are like a couple of MAGNETS
– move away from each other.
And whoever's making that hissing
sound please STOP right now."

I gave Marcus a LOOK and whispered,

"That would be YOU then."

Mr Fullerman heard me.

"Do you need some help, Tom?"

"Not really, sir."

"Excellent, that's music to my ears. I'll
look forward to seeing ALL your
maths completed then," Mr Fullerman

said, and he carried on marking our work.

Marcus moved away and left me in peace for a while. 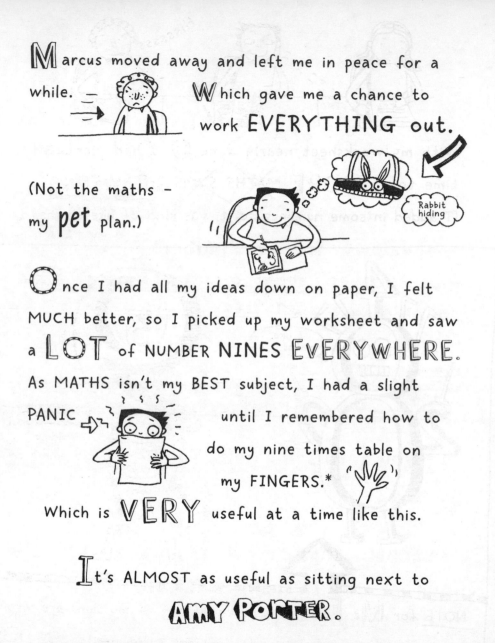 **W**hich gave me a chance to work EVERYTHING out.

(Not the maths – my **pet** plan.)

Rabbit hiding

Once I had all my ideas down on paper, I felt MUCH better, so I picked up my worksheet and saw a **LOT** of NUMBER NINES EVERYWHERE.

As MATHS isn't my BEST subject, I had a slight PANIC until I remembered how to do my nine times table on my FINGERS.*

Which is VERY useful at a time like this.

It's ALMOST as useful as sitting next to AMY PORTER.

* See pages 228-229 on how to do your nine times table on your fingers.

With my worksheet nearly done 😊 I had plenty of
time to do MORE ~~MATHS~~ ~~SUMS~~ DRAWINGS.
(I added in some <u>numbers</u>, so it was kind of like maths.)

Number
creature

I like
maths.

Big
number

DOGZOMBIE
holding a
9 and a 3

NOTE for Mr Fullerman – sorry if any of my sums are wrong.
I hope these good drawings help me get some merits. 😊 😀

For the rest of the day all I could think about
was having a **pet**, right up until the bell went.

Even on the walk home I found myself looking

at other people's dogs and imagining

they were mine.

I WAS going to tell Mum and Dad about Mark's **pet** as soon as I got back. But instead I found myself wandering around the house doing other VERY important things like:

STARING AT THE WALL.

Picking bits of FLUFF off my trousers.

Flicking the bits of fluff to see how far they would FLY.

(Not that far.)

What if Mum and Dad said NO about the **pet?** That would be really AWKWARD and I wouldn't be happy about it either. Mark said he'd come to see me straight after school, so I was running out of time to ask them. After a bit more FLUFF finding...

EVENTUALLY ⇨

I stood right in front of them and

BLURTED out...

"Mum and Dad, can I ask you a QUESTION?"
(They both did a RAISED EYEBROW LOOK.)

"Go on..." Mum said suspiciously.

"WELL, my friend Mark Clump has asked me to do him a really HUGE favour. AND because I'm a NICE person and I always try and do good things, I told him not to worry because of COURSE I could take one of his pets just for a few days to help him out."
(I whispered the word "pets" really softly hoping they might miss it.) ☺

"That's nice of you, Tom," Dad said.

PHEW! That was EASY.

I followed up *quickly* by saying...

"THANK YOU! THAT'S BRILLIANT!
Mark's on his way over right now and he'll be
VERY happy."

Hang on a second. Did you just say ➡ PET?

(Trust Mum to hear with her BAT ears.)

"Maybe..."

Before she could say NO to me, I found another
way to ask the same question...

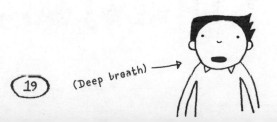

(19) (Deep breath) →

PLEAse PLEASE Please
Please! PLEASE please
PLEASE! Please Please
PLease PLEASE Please
please PLEASE! PLEASE
PLEASE please PLEASE
PLEASe please PLEASE
PLease PLEASE!

Please PLEASE...

I only stopped saying PLEASE when I ran out of breath, which gave Mum the chance to JUMP in and say...

"You KNOW we can't have **pets** in the house, Tom."

"But Mark said <u>his</u> granny can't look after any more of his **pets** and his mum was ALL **stressed out!**"

I did an impression of Mark's mum being **stressed.** (It's just a WILD guess if she really looks like this.)

"I was only trying to be HELPFUL," I added in a sad voice.

"I'm not surprised Mark's mum is **stressed** with all those **pets** in the house," Dad said.

"EXACTLY!"

"Is everything OK with Mark and his family then?" Mum wanted to know.

21

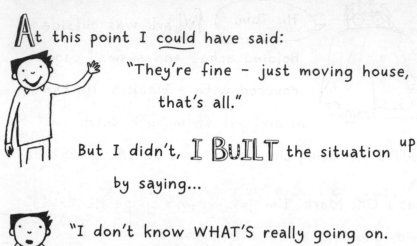

At this point I could have said:

"They're fine - just moving house, that's all."

But I didn't, I BUILT the situation ᵘᴾ by saying...

"I don't know WHAT'S really going on. But Mark asked for my help and I'm his friend."

Which was true, though I made it sound a lot more

⚡ DRAMATIC ⚡ than it really was.

"I'm still not sure, Tom. What if..." Mum started to say when the doorbell RANG.

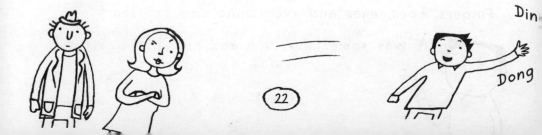

Din

Dong

Hi, Tom. **M**ark was outside holding a bag and a small cage covered with a blanket. He came in and put them both down.

"THANKS for doing this, Tom. You're a REAL LIFESAVER."

"That's OK, Mark. I'm just trying to be HELPFUL," I said, glancing at Mum and Dad to make a point. Changing their minds would be lot harder to do now Mark was actually here. UNLESS there was something DODGY lurking under that blanket like:

A MASSIVE SPIDER

A **skunk** (pongy)

Millions of cockroaches

Fingers, toes, eyes and everything else crossed it was something cute and nice like a DOG!

"**My** granny's waiting for me outside, so I can't stay for long. But she's VERY pleased there's one less animal in her house — even for a short time," Mark told us.

"I bet she is," Dad said.

All I REALLY wanted to know was ...

WHAT WAS THE PET?

Mark started to look in the bag and said, "Hang on, I just need to sort out his toys..."

TOYS! MARK SAID TOYS!

A DOG HAS TOYS.

YES! YES! "Is it a DOG?"

"Oh, didn't I tell you what it was?" Mark asked me.

"NO!"

we all said together.

"Sorry about that."

Mark took the blanket off the cage

AND INSIDE ...

... there wasn't a dog.

Or if it WAS a dog, it was a teeny-weeny one.

(Sigh.)

"He's asleep right now. But don't worry, when **Marble** wakes up he'll get a lot more lively, I PROMISE."

"What IS **Marble?**"

I asked (trying not to sound too disappointed).

"He's a HAMSTER."

Mark could tell by my expression that I wasn't sure about a hamster.

"Hamsters are VERY good **pets**. He likes to store snacks inside his cheeks for later."

"That's handy," I said.

I suppose ANY **pet** is better than no **pet** at all and Mum and Dad seemed OK about **Marble.**

Which was a good thing. ☺

Before Mark left, he gave me instructions on how to look after **Marble** and clean his cage.

"Watch out when you change his bedding – he likes to try and go for a walk. You have to keep an EYE on him," Mark warned me.

Yippee!

"Do you mean he ESCAPES?"

"Sometimes. But he's not that fast and usually doesn't get very far."

"HOW far?" Mum wanted to know.

"You can always get him back with these special hamster treats."
Mark held up a packet of hamster nibbles.

"I won't let him out of my sight," I assured him.

"I'll pick **Marble** up in a week if that's OK?"

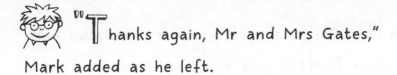 "**T**hanks again, Mr and Mrs Gates,"
Mark added as he left.

"He's **S**○ polite. It's nice you can help him, Tom,"
Mum said once he'd gone –
like it was HER idea!
(Groan.)

"You'll have to keep **Marble** in your room
away from Delia," Dad told me,
just as Delia arrived home.
He quickly put the blanket over **Marble's**
cage and moved it out of her way.

 "**WHAT'S** going on?"

"It's not for long. Tom's friend is picking
him up in a few days' time. You won't even
know he's here!" Mum tried to reassure Delia
(which CLEARLY wasn't working).

"Pick WHAT up?"

Delia said, looking confused.

"It's just a little hamster - nothing to worry about," Mum told her.

He's not *THAT* little,

I said, because the cage looked quite big.

"WHY has Tom got a PET? You know I can't be near them!"

Delia said, waving her arms around and being all CROSS.

"I'll have to go and stay at AVRIL'S with all that ANIMAL FUR flying everywhere."

"If you keep away from Tom's room you'll be fine. He's not going to escape, is he, Tom?"

Dad said, wanting to reassure Delia.

"**H**e might ESCAPE. You never know,"

I said, stirring things up a bit.

"This is RIDICULOUS!"

Delia stamped her foot.

STAMP

"We'll make sure he doesn't get free, won't

we, TOM?" Mum said, doing the eyebrow thing again.

"YES. But it will HELP if you STAY AWAY

from ME and my room,"

I told Delia with a nice smile.

(STAY-AWAY hand)

ME

THIS IS ☆BRILLIANT!☆

Delia

(Big distance.)

Delia can't bother me at all – it's **OFFICIAL.**

I won't even mind cleaning out **Marble's** cage

because everything about having a **pet** is going to be

FANTASTIC FUN, I can tell. ☺ I'm enjoying myself

already and he's only been here a few moments.

I take **Marble** up to my room to get him settled (even though he's asleep).

I watch him doing nothing for a while. ☺ He's still asleep when Mum and Dad come in to say goodnight and check everything is OK.

"Don't let **Marble** out of his cage," Dad says.

"I won't."

"No comics or turning the lights back on either," Mum adds, tucking me into bed.

"Night!" I say, and I wait until they're downstairs ... before turning on my BOOK LIGHT and climbing out of bed, because I THINK ...

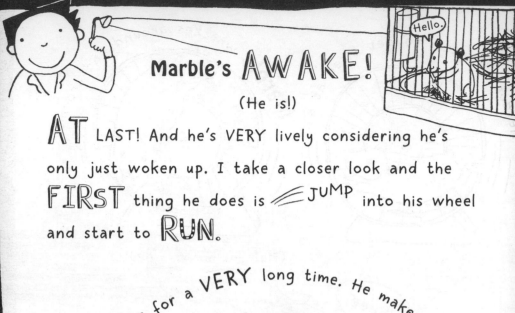

Marble's AWAKE!

(He is!)

AT LAST! And he's VERY lively considering he's only just woken up. I take a closer look and the FIRST thing he does is JUMP into his wheel and start to RUN.

Marble keeps running for a VERY long time. He makes the wheel spin really FAST...

Marble decides to go on his see-saw. He shuffles from one end to the other to make it go UP⬆ and down... UP⬆ and down.

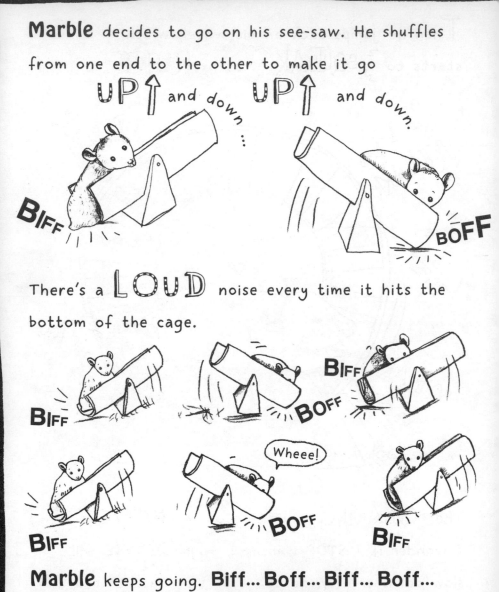

BIFF

BOFF

There's a LOUD noise every time it hits the bottom of the cage.

BIFF

BOFF

BIFF

BIFF

Wheee!

BOFF

BIFF

Marble keeps going. **Biff... Boff... Biff... Boff... Biff... Boff... Biff... Boff... Biff... Boff...**

Then he jumps back on his wheel, which starts to SQUEAK as he RUNS.

The SQUEAKING is getting on my NERVES. I wonder if I STOP watching, maybe **Marble** will slow down or even go to sleep? I go back to bed and close my eyes. But **Marble** just keeps on running.

ALL NIGHT LONG.

SQUEA

SQUEAK!

SQUEAK!

SQUEA

It keeps me awake until the light starts to creep through my curtains as the SUN comes up. THEN finally the SQUEAKING slows down and

STOPS.

I'm just beginning
to drift off to sleep.

AT LAST.

Sigh...

ZZZZZZZZZZZZZ

ZZZZZZZZZZZZZ

I WASN'T EXPECTING my cuckoo clock to do THAT! I thought it was **BROKEN.** All that fiddling around and WINDING it up I'd done trying to fix it must have worked.

I drag the clock out from under the bed to make it STOP. I'm SO TIRED – I can't believe it's morning already. **Marble** is still asleep and hasn't moved at all despite the NOISE.

 (Lucky **Marble.**)

Though it sounds like Delia's AWAKE too. I can hear her grumbling and COMPLAINING from her bedroom. She doesn't sound happy at ALL.

(Uh-oh...)

THAT STUPID CUCKOO CLOCK! Grrrrrrr...

I can't believe it's WOKEN me UP! AGAIN!

The **only** thing that would ANNOY Delia even MORE than my  CUCKOO clock going off would be ME sneaking into the bathroom *Grrrrrr* before her. (She HATES that.)

Despite being half asleep, I make an E X T R A effort to creep down the corridor and keep up this ☆FUN☆ family tradition.

Evidence

SLAM

TOM!

Besides, it's a good idea to be early for school, as Mr Fullerman is on a MISSION to make sure we all get to class ON TIME. He's put up a **NEW CHART** called

Listen up, you lot!

CLASS 5F

IT'S NOT GREAT TO BE LATE.

Group 1	Group 2	Group 3	Group 4

He told us,

There's FAR too much DAWDLING in the corridors. You all need to get to your lessons on time!

But it's SO easy to get distracted on the way to class by things like:

- Friends

  Skill.

  No hands!

- Champ (and other games...)

- Following teachers (for a DARE).

(Brave!)

(Super brave!)

The [NEW CHART] is supposed to encourage ALL of us NOT TO BE LATE.

Mr Fullerman divided the whole class into four groups. Just for a change, I'm not with Marcus.

Group 1 ↑ Group 2

Each group starts with 50 points and if you're late – your group loses a POINT. The group with the MOST points at the end of each month gets a

SPECIAL TREAT! (Which sounds promising.)

Though Mr Fullerman hasn't told us what the "treat" actually is YET – he says it's a

SURPRISE!

So that's another good reason to get to the BATHROOM first. I'm still sleepy, but knowing how much it will annoy Delia perks me up. I just have to remember to LOCK the bathroom door.

CLICK   (ALL done.)

When I look at myself in the bathroom mirror

I get a bit of a

SHOCK.

Where are my EYES? They've disappeared somewhere into my FACE.

I look like a POTATO.

(This could be a BIG problem at school.)

I NEVER expected looking after a **pet** would be **THIS** tiring. Maybe if I put a flannel soaked in COLD water on my face, it might wake me UP.

(It's the kind of thing Mum would do.)

I don't want Delia to see my potato face either, because she will:

1. LAUGH! Ha! Ha!

2. Guess why I'm tired.

Marble kept you awake.

No he didn't!

3. Tell Mum and Dad about **Marble.**

That pet's TROUBLE.

We suspected.

THEN Mum and Dad will send **Marble** back to Mark's.

Off you go.

Which would be a DISASTER!

So I give my face a good SCRUB and hope it works. No need to have a SHOWER or do anything DRASTIC like that.

I'm just drying off when Delia starts knocking on the door. (Loudly.) She's SNEEZING too.

atishoooooo!

Then she says,

> Your clock is SO annoying, Tom.
>
> Don't take AGES in there.
>
> ## HURRY UP, WILL YOU?
>
> (Sniff...)

Sniff

The moment she tells me to HURRY UP ... I SLOW down.

(Just for fun.)

Slow motion

TOM, I know you're not having a shower or WASHING!

"I might be having a shower OR a BATH. How do you know?"

I shout through the door.

DO **NOT** have a bath. I don't want to be late. I'm going to count to **TEN.**

At some point I will have to leave the bathroom and Delia will probably try and do that ANNOYING HAIR RUFFLE thing on me (or worse).

I'm trying to THINK of what I can do when she starts counting...

I'm WAITING. ONE ... TWO ... THREE ... FOUR ...

I'm a bit STUCK (and still thinking...) when suddenly I spot ...

... a LAUNDRY BASKET  on the floor

that's about the same size as **Marble's** cage.

I COULD pretend that **Marble's** with me,

and then Delia would HAVE to stay out of my way,

OR at least move. I cover the basket with the

towel and then I give her a

WARNING.

"I'll come out **IF** YOU GO AWAY, DELIA."

(Delia starts RATTLING the door handle.)

"I've got **MARBLE** with me so you'd better

give me some S P A C E .

Don't say I didn't

WARN YOU."

You're **NOT** supposed to take THAT **pet** out of your ROOM, TOM!

"His name is **MARBLE** and I was giving him a TOUR of the house. He's not been here before and he's a GUEST. AND I wasn't expecting to bump into YOU."

Nice place.

You'll be in TROUBLE when Mum and Dad find out you're taking him for WALKS.

Delia sounds **CROSS**, so it's only a matter of time before Mum or Dad will want to know what's going on. I decide to make my move, so I open the door a tiny bit and PEEK outside.

Then I hold the basket in front of me and say, "Coming through –

BACK AWAY, DELIA."

It's like I've got a MAGIC force field protecting me, which is FANTASTIC!

I wish I had this all the time.

I'm about to get to the safety of my room when Mum and Dad both appear and stop me.

"Your face looks a bit red, Tom," Mum says, and does a cheek SQUEEZE on me, which doesn't really help.

"You don't feel HOT. You've been rough with a flannel again, haven't you?"

"NO," I say, wondering HOW she always knows exactly what I've been doing.

Grrrr

No
hat

"WHY all the shouting, you two?" Dad wants to know. I'm just hoping they'll BOTH ignore the towel on the basket and not ask me any AWKWARD questions.

"And what's under the towel, Tom?"

(Too late.)

Before I can THINK of something to say, Delia is already shouting.

Tom, you promised!

IT'S THE HAMSTER. That's why I'm CROSS.

Mum says sternly. I try and explain in a whisper so Delia can't hear me.

"It's just a laundry basket. **Marble's** in his cage."

Dad goes into my room and says,

TOM, where's **Marble?** He's not in HERE!

Which gives Delia a chance to say AGAIN,

Tom's got him!

(This isn't working out like I planned at all.)

I'm forced to abandon the basket and run into my room to show Dad that **Marble** is still there.

"He's not in his cage.

Did you close it properly? I can't see him anywhere.

Is that **Marble's** food on the floor?"

Dad's looking for **Marble** under my BED!

"No, they're my biscuit crumbs," I tell him.

Mum walks in and starts moving chairs around and

getting all worried as well.

"I KNEW this would happen," she sighs.

While they're both FREAKING out I

take another LOOK in **Marble's** cage.

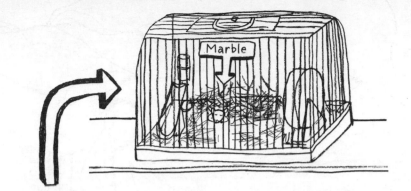

"DAD, he's THERE — I TOLD you he was!"

"Well, he wasn't a second ago, I can promise you that." Dad squints at **Marble** like he's checking it's really him. *Hmmm*

"That's a relief," Mum says. "Now it's time to get ready for school," she adds as Delia STOMPS past my room and tells me grumpily,

Keep that hamster away from me, TOM!

"SHHHHHHHHHHHHHHHHHHH! You'll wake **Marble** up!" I say cheerily as she heads to the bathroom. Though looking at **Marble** right now I'm not sure ANYTHING could wake him.

At least my EYES have opened a bit more after all the excitement (and cold flannel). Getting ready for school is a LOT quicker now I can see properly.

BEFORE flannel	AFTER flannel
Potato-face.	Not a potato-face.

I'm hoping that today at school will be

EASY-PEASY with nothing **too** difficult that makes me feel even more tired than I am right now.

Here's a list of things I need to avoid:

1. Running
2. ~~ANY~~ ~~Spelling~~ tests
3. ~~ANY~~ ~~Tricky~~ maths
4. Champ
5. Concentrating
6. Marcus (especially if he's being annoying)

I could go on.

While Dad was looking under my bed for **Marble,** I spotted a fully wrapped **CHOCOLATE FROG.** Which I'm definitely going to eat (obviously), but not right now. I'll save it for later.

After breakfast (and a BITE of **frog –** I couldn't wait) I'm about to head over to **D**erek's when Mum tells me I should take my new raincoat with me. I say, OK! then sneak another nibble of **frog** (without Mum seeing).

Derek won't mind being early for school either as his class have to pick up litter if they're late. I also give him a piece of my frog, which he's happy about as well.

Derek's my best friend after all.

Thanks, Tom!

Eat it slowly!

We take our time walking to school so we can chat about **DOGZOMBIES**.

I tell him about **Marble** keeping me awake all night too.

"What's with the tiny eyes?" Derek asks.

"All hamsters have tiny eyes."

Tiny eyes

"I meant YOUR eyes - not the hamster's," Derek LAUGHs.

"You should have seen them earlier," I say, and I show Derek what I mean.

"I wish I could stay home and catch up on my sleep - like **Marble's** doing right now."

Yum...

"Rooster chews stuff when I'm not there."

"We should write a song about Rooster," I suggest.

"We should," Derek says, but we can't think of any ideas so I divide up the last two bits of **frog** (which hasn't lasted as long as I thought).

Meanwhile – back at home ⇨

Being really early for school means we're the FIRST kids here. Normally I'm in a BIG *hurry* and *rushing* around so this feels odd.

It's like I've come to school on a weekend by mistake. (That's happened before.)

Where is everyone?

The good news is we can sit on the BEST bench all by ourselves.

"No litter picking for me today," Derek says.

"Or late marks either," I tell Derek. Then he suggests we do something NOW that's really important.

"We've finished the **chocolate frog** - sorry."

"No, not that."

"OK," I say, trying to THINK what he's going to say.

"We need to plan ..."

WORLD DOMINATION FOR DOGZOMBIES

YES!

Along with **N**orman,  we've decided that if we're EVER going to be the BEST band in the world, we'll have to do something more than just play at Leafy Green Old Folks' Home.

(Not that there's anything wrong with that.)

We should make a music video,

Derek suggests,
which is an EXCELLENT idea. ☺
(We've made one before – a while ago.)

"What do we do first?" I ask **D**erek.

"We need NEW songs. I've got some ideas if you want to see them." (I do.)

"A new song to go with the video would be good."

"It would."

Derek gets out a notebook, which has lots of RANDOM stuff in it.

"Does that say 'I like GOATS'?" I ask, as that seems like an odd thing to write a song about.

"It's my wobbly handwriting. It says BOATS," Derek explains, which makes more sense. (Sort of.)

SONG IDEAS FOR DOGZOMBIES
I LIKE TREATS
I LIKE BOATS
DOGS - song about a dog?
NO to HOMEWORK
Pencils BOO!
Ladders Climbing up

I have a {think} and then try singing a few lines...

"I'm a GOAT,

I live on a BOAT,

I wear a RAINCOAT!"

(Unlike [me,] as I forgot to bring mine.)

"It's a HIT!" Derek LAUGHS and turns

over a new page in his notebook to write it down.

"What else shall we add?" he asks me.

Hmmmmm   Hmmmmm

Hmmmmm   Hmmmmm

    "Let's come back to it later," Derek suggests.

Getting words mixed up (like goat and boat)

reminds me of something I like to do in assembly.

I tell Derek,

    "You know that song – the one that goes

    like this..." (I'm going to sing again.)

"Let's ALL STAND UP AND *LOUDLY* SING!"

"I know that song."

"Well I always change the words to:

"Let's ALL STAND UP FOR DOODLING!"

"That's brilliant," Derek LAUGHS.

We make a PACT that we'll BOTH sing those words.

"No one will notice – you'll see!"

I tell Derek confidently.

We carry on trying to work on our own songs, which isn't going that well.

Hmmmmm
Hmmmmm
Hmmmmm
Hmmmmm

"I've got an idea!" I say after a while. "The NEXT person who walks into school – we'll put them in our song."

"OK," Derek says.

We wait ... and wait ... and wait ... →
until Mrs Worthington arrives.
Neither of us can think
of a word that rhymes
with moustache. So we
see who else turns up.

You're early, boys!

Derek suddenly starts writing stuff down, and crossing things out. Writing – crossing – writing – crossing – writing...

"I've had a song idea!"

Then he reads out...

"School in the morning...
There's no one around."

Which is TRUE and a good start. I try and think
of the NEXT line. (Songwriting face)

It's SO early and you can't hear a T~~EACHER~~
↓ Pigeon
SOUND,
Sitting on a BENCH with nothing to ~~EAT~~ PROVE.

"GENIUS - I'll write that down too," Derek says.
"This is like a proper song now. It's going to
be BRILLIANT," I say, and then we congratulate
ourselves with a fist bump.

Derek writes it all out nicely and so far our song goes like this... School in the morning,
There's no one around,
It's so early,
You can't hear a sound,
Sitting on a bench
With nothing to PROVE.

(Songs don't have to rhyme but **DOGZOMBIES** ones usually do. This is where it gets tricky.)

"What rhymes with PROVE?" I wonder.

"How about HOOVE – or BOOVE?" Derek adds, but I'm not sure they're even real words. We write down the alphabet to help us.

A B C D E F G H I J K L M N O P Q R S T U V W X Y Z

```
o       o
o       o        But we're rudely interrupted by a
v       v
e       e        group of younger kids, who say...
```

Huh?

Can you MOVE to another bench, please?

"HEY, that's it! MOVE rhymes with PROVE!"

Derek says and writes that down too.

"YES it does!" (We are songwriting geniuses.)
The kids are still waiting for us to go.

"Could you both sit somewhere else?"

she says again.

"Why do we have to MOVE?"
I say, looking at the empty school grounds.

"OK, don't then. We'll just dance around you."

"What dance?"

"This one – for SHAKE and WAKE.
You can join in if you want?"

"We'll see," Derek says.
We try and ignore the kids once

they start dancing.

70

Which isn't easy.

Everyone **SHAKE AND WAKE!** PUT YOUR ARMS UP!

Now dip down. Do the Charleston! Do the Charleston!

REACH UP HIGH! WAVE your ARMS in the AIR like you just don't care!

Jump UP! Jump UP!

They do the WHOLE dance TWICE.

"Come on, you two! Join in!" the girl says.

Reluctantly, we WAVE our arms around just to stop them BUGGING us.

Once they finish LEAPING around, Derek and I grab our bags and make a *DASH* for another bench.

"Phew. That was embarrassing," Derek says.

"At least there weren't too many kids around to see us looking like TWITS!" I add.

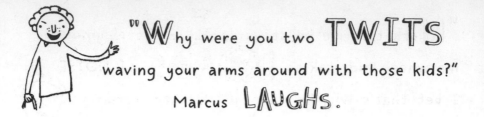

"**W**hy were you two TWITS waving your arms around with those kids?" Marcus LAUGHS.

"They were dancing around uS,"

I point out. Trust Marcus to see everything. I don't really want to talk about dancing – especially with Marcus – so I change the subject fast.

"I've got Mark's **pet** now."

"Was it a snake? Stick insects? Beetles?"

"He's got **pet** beetles?"

(Why am I surprised?)

Pets

"He's got LOADS.

What did you get, then?"

That's me!

"I've got his hamster – **Marble.**"

Marcus starts LAUGHING!

"Mark told me he stays up ALL night playing in his wheel and making LOADS of NOISE. I bet that's why he gave you his hamster!"

I find myself sticking UP for **Marble** and saying, "NO, he sleeps really well."

(Which is true – just not at night.)

"After a few days you'll be WISHING you did have the snake after all." Marcus starts doing that stupid ARM thing and hissssssing at me.

"That's annoying," Derek says.

Hissssssssss

So far my EASY-PEASY day at school

isn't quite working out like I expected.

This morning we've got assembly, so I'm going to sit next to my mate **S**olid because:

1. We can have a catch-up.

2. He's very **TALL** and good for hiding behind.

3. Which will be very useful if I get tired and need to close my eyes for a sneaky rest.

Mr **F**ullerman tells us that **M**rs **N**ap has an important **ANNOUNCEMENT** to make today.

"Get ready for a musical TREAT!"

He's doing his best to make it sound exciting.

(I think I know what it is.)

Here's my →  ⟵ "I'M THRILLED" face.

With the **WHOLE** school sitting and
waiting to hear the **BIG NEWS**,
Mrs Nap plays a jolly tune on the piano.

"Hello, everyone!
Today children from class
2D will be showing you our
new FUN and HEALTHY way
to start the DAY! It's called

SHAKE and WAKE!"

(I knew it!)

"Every class will get the chance to create their
own routine and then teach it to all of us. Today
it's 2D's turn – with the help of a few volunteers!"
As the kids from 2D stand up, I avoid eye contact
and use Solid for cover. I don't want them to see ME!

I think I'm safe... – phew

Turns out I'm not.

I pick YOU!

Solid's not safe either. Derek's lucky he's not in my class. I can see him waving at me.

And Marcus too. Ha!Ha! (Sigh ... here goes.)

SHAKE and WAKE!

At least it doesn't last too long.

As we sit down Mr Keen congratulates us.

"WELL DONE! **SHAKE and WAKE!** will take place by the benches in the school grounds every week. So all of you can join in next time – with music! And speaking of music..."

Mrs Nap begins to play the piano again.

I recognize the song – it's the "Let's Stand Up for Doodling" one. I give Derek a SIGN and whisper to Solid, "Listen to this!"

I start with a quiet...

> Let's stand up for doodling...

While everyone else sings,

"Let's stand up and loudly sing."

Then I do it AGAIN.

> Let's stand up for doodling...!

A few more kids join in ... then a few more ... and a few more. Until loads of children are all singing,

"Let's stand up for doodling!"

It's THE ONLY THING YOU CAN HEAR!

The WHOLE school is singing...

Let's stand UP for DOODLING!

I think it's
BRILLIANT!

Mrs Nap and Mr Keen don't agree.

"Did you notice something unusual about that song, Mr Keen?"

"I did, Mrs Nap."

Mr Keen doesn't look very happy.

"If YOU were the person who started singing the WRONG words to the song – DON'T do it again. You know who you are."

I keep looking ahead and try not to react too much.

How could they know it was me? I should be OK.

No one says anything.

Because they don't have to.

I'm trying to EXPLAIN to Mr Fullerman how I accidentally sang the wrong words. "I just got muddled up! Sorry, sir – it's hard to get them out of my HEAD now."

He makes me promise NOT to do it again.

As IF today couldn't get any WORSE, he then asks me WHERE my **MYSTERY STORY** homework is?

I have to STOP myself from saying, ("MYSTERY", sir,) because I haven't done it YET and

I'll get into MORE trouble. As I'm thinking about what I should say Mr Fullerman adds,

"Come on, Tom, I've heard EVERY excuse going so far. Dogs, washing machines, even ALIENS. WHAT'S NEXT?"

Just as he says that a HUGE BOLT of Lightning gives us all ... ➡

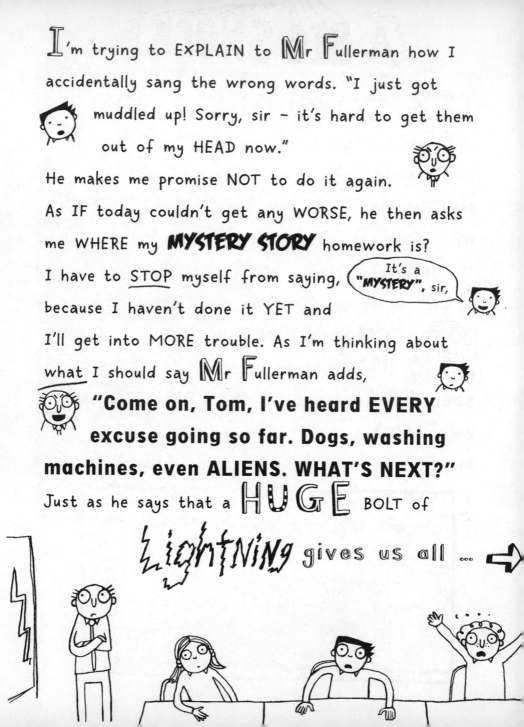

A BIG SHOCK

IT'S SO SUPER LOUD,

and good timing too as it makes Mr Fullerman

forget about my homework (for now).

Brad Galloway shouts out, "It's a GHOST!"

Which makes the whole class go CRAZY!

Then hailstones start hitting the windows and we

all get out of our seats to take a LOOK.

"CALM DOWN, everyone,"

Mr Fullerman tells us. **"You've all**

seen thunderstorms before."

We have ... but not like THIS.

There's another BIG flash of lightning ...

AGHHH!

... and all the LIGHTS go **OUT** in the classroom!

"THIS IS **SPOOKY!**" Brad Galloway

SHOUTS, making things seem a lot WORSE!

"SIT DOWN, PLEASE. The lights will be back on soon," Mr Fullerman tries to

reassure us.

It's very **GLOOMY** and dark now. Norman

starts pretending he can't see anything at ALL.

"Where's EVERYONE GONE?"

Then someone else makes some NIGHT

OWL noises. Whooooo Whooooooo

"That's enough wildlife, class 5F. It's not that dark," Mr Fullerman says, but he's

trying not to LAUGH.

Then Mr Sprocket comes in from next door's

classroom and tells us,

"Sit tight - no need to worry, we've just had a

POWER CUT in the

WHOLE school and some of the streets around us too."

WOW, this is the MOST exciting thing that's happened for a long time!

(Apart from when we had a fire drill and Marcus didn't have time to change out of his PE kit – that was **FUNNY!**)

The good news for me is with a slightly darker classroom I get to close my eyes for a sneaky rest.

But that doesn't last long.

"We're going to carry on with our lesson until everything's fixed."

(Shame.)

"But, sir, no one can SEE anything!" Julia Morton says. (She's got a point.)

"I'm going to read one of the BEST MYSTERY HOMEWORK stories to you, so all you have to do is pay attention and listen," Mr Fullerman says.

(Brilliant ... time for a rest then!)

Who Stole the Cake?

By Florence Mitchell

MONSTERS really do exist. I know this because I've seen them, mostly at night sneaking around looking for something to EAT. It's also TRUE that **MONSTERS** HIDE in dark cupboards and under children's beds. They stay very still until you're asleep and then crawl out to MESS up your toys. **MONSTERS** are always hungry and steal as much food as they can. A **MONSTER'S** favourite food is cake, and they will always SNIFF it out if you try and hide it.

SNIFF
SNIFF

If you want to SEE a **MONSTER** all you have to do is bake a cake – or maybe even lots of cakes. Leave them in your kitchen and the monster will be SURE to find them. It will LuRK somewhere dark until you've gone.

Then it will come out and SCOFF as many cakes as it can before anyone finds it. With huge eyes, massive sharp teeth, fierce claws and hairy bodies, **MONSTERS** can be scary. How do I know all this about **MONSTERS,** you might be wondering?

That's easy...

I am a MONSTER

(and I stole your cake).

Did you enjoy that, Class 5F?

Florence's story was **SCARIER** than expected. The sound of the caretaker's keys jangling away outside in the corridor doesn't help. He's running around trying to fix things, which isn't working as we're still sitting in a **GLOOMY** classroom. Mr Fullerman wants to read us another story. **"This one's called 'THE MYSTERY OF THE SHADOW',** he says just as the door begins to s l o w l y **CREAK** open.

"It's a GHOST!"
Brad Galloway shouts.

(It's not.)

It's Mrs Mumble.

(Who's not that scary — most of the time.)

Hello, Mr Fullerman, I have some NEWS for you. Due to the POWER CUT I'm afraid the school will have to CLOSE. I'm sorry to interrupt your lesson - but you'll all be going home EARLY.

YEAH!

(No one looks unhappy, especially not ME!)

Those of you who can't go home, don't worry, because Blue Coat School have NOT had a power cut – so you'll be able to go there to wait instead. Which is VERY helpful for all of us.

I'm not going to Blue Coat School, that's for sure.

(It's HOME TIME for ME!)

Blue Coat School isn't far away from ours. We often have to play them at sport – well, I don't. But if you're in the football, basketball OR netball team you do. They USUALLY win, which can get a bit boring if you have to watch.

They also have a VERY FANCY official school mascot AND a SPECIAL song they like to sing to keep their team going. Oakfield never used to have ANYTHING like that, although I did make up a chant once when Norman was playing them at football. It had crying actions and EVERYTHING.

Oakfield School,
You can do it.
One more goal,
Let's go to it.
Blue Coat School,
Your team is BAD.
When you lose
You'll be SAD...

I thought it was REALLY GOOD!
Some of the teachers didn't agree,
including Mr Keen.

Tom!

I stopped singing when Blue Coat School scored
10 goals against us and it
didn't make sense any more.

Oakfield School	Blue Coat School
1	10

After that match
some of the school council
kids suggested that Oakfield School should
have their OWN mascot to wave around.
Mr Keen agreed and thought it was a good idea.

Good idea! So the school ran a competition to
design a NEW MASCOT. Lots of kids
entered (including me) and there was a big display
of all the entries pinned up round the hall.

Tom Gates (Mine didn't win.)

Two ideas got the most votes and TIED for first
place. The school council kids had a BRAINWAVE and
decided that BOTH designs should win.

Which would have been OK if they hadn't cut the drawings in half and STUCK them together to make a NEW and slightly ODD mascot. One of the parents

offered to SEW it together, and when it was finished the school council kids wanted to do a BIG REVEAL in assembly. They covered the winning mascot with a tablecloth and when they took it AWAY...

This mascot is called... (Wait for it.)

There was a **HUGE** GASP – followed by LOTS of LAUGHING because no one was expecting the mascot to look like THAT!

The school council kids told everyone,
  "It's called Big Ugly Monster!"
But Mr Keen noticed what the initials spelt out
and suggested they rename it OAKY instead.
(They didn't have much choice.) But the funny thing
is, EVER since we've had OAKY, we've been winning
LOADS more sports matches. EVEN against Blue
Coat School. Norman thinks WAVING
it around puts the other teams off
because it looks SO WEIRD.

I'm **glad** I won't have to go to Blue Coat School. It will be more ☆**FUN**☆ seeing **Marble** (unless he's still asleep).

The school office does a **BIG** CHECK on who's allowed home and who's not. **Mr Fullerman** has a LIST and is about to READ it out. I begin getting my stuff together when I hear him say,

TOM GATES – Blue Coat School.

"WHAT? There MUST be a MISTAKE! My dad's at home," I tell **Mr Fullerman** quickly.

"Sorry Tom, it says here you'll be picked up from Blue Coat."

No WAY!

Ha! Ha!

AMY sees that I'm in a **PANIC** and she asks me if I want to go to HER house. I don't really have time to THINK too much.

I just say,

"YES PLEASE - that's great, THANKS, AMY."

"OK, Tom, I'll ask Mrs Mumble to contact your mum or dad," Mr Fullerman

tells me, so that's something. I have to wait to find out if it's OK.

I've only ever been to AMY's house once for her birthday party, when she invited the WHOLE class. We played pin the tail on the donkey, only I kept missing and popped loads of balloons instead.

Amy says she doesn't mind waiting for me, unlike Marcus who keeps saying... "I'm allowed HOME - Ha! Ha!"

To fill up the time and take my mind off the possibility of being FORCED to go to Blue Coat School, I do a doodle. (It's a bit scary looking because Florence's story is still in my HEAD!)

GOOD NEWS! Marcus has stopped

bugging me and gone home. (At LAST.)

Then **Mr Fullerman** tells me...

 **"Tom – it's fine for you to go to Amy's. Your mum called and said your dad will pick you up later."**

`BRILLIANT!`

I don't know why Dad's NOT at home – but it

doesn't matter now. I get my things

together as **AMY**'s waiting.

"Let's GO!" I say cheerily when Florence and

Indrani come and join us.

"We're READY as well," they say.

(Which is a surprise.)

"Great – we can all walk to my house," **AMY** says.

"TOGETHER?" (I didn't know Florence and Indrani

were coming too.)

 "I won't be staying LONG – my dad's picking
me up," I explain as I follow them out.

Caretaker Stan is making sure we all leave carefully.

"Mind how you go - it's a bit DARK with no lights."

I'm squinting in the gloomy corridor when Norman bumps into ME! (Which isn't unusual.)

Whoops!

But it does give me the chance to tell him about doing a **DOGZOMBIES** video.

He says, "GREAT! Count me in!"

But I know I'll have to remind him again.

(He won't remember.)

AMY, Florence and Indrani are chatting a lot as we all walk back to her house. I'm LISTENING to them talk about their homework and WHEN they're going to do it. There's no mention of SNACKS or anything important like THAT.

(Which is weird.)

Chat!

Chat!

Chat!

Chat!

When we get to **AMY**'s house, straight
away her mum says to ME...

"The last time I saw you, Tom, was on holiday at the
PINE TREE RIVIERA. Did you enjoy yourself?"

I start to remember some of the things that happened.
"Ummmm... MOSTLY," I say. THEN I tell them
about how Dad got me to CLIMB through an open
window of our villa.

"It was the WRONG ONE - but we stayed there
for NEARLY a **WHOLE** WEEK anyway!" I explain.

"In someone else's villa?" **AMY'S** mum asks.

"Sort of."

Everyone seems quite surprised.

(Maybe I shouldn't have mentioned that BIT.)

 Then Florence wants to know,

"Who's looking forward to doing the

SHAKE AND WAKE! this week?"

Indrani looks at **ME** and says,

"Tom, you already know what to do – you can SHOW US!"

(I'm not KEEN on that idea.)

Florence waves her ARMS around.

– Ha! Ha!

"Does it go like THIS?"

I pretend I can't remember.

(Maybe I should have gone to

Blue Coat School after all.)

I am SAVED by **AMY**'s mum, who appears with

a plate of sandwiches.

"Who's HUNGRY?" she asks.

"**I AM!**"

I shout enthusiastically.

Then I calm down a bit and add, "PLEASE."

AMY's mum puts the plate

on the table and tells us all,

"HELP yourselves!"

So I do....

BUT IT'S TUÑA.

I HATE TUNA.

So I kind of let my mouth hang open and do a great big **COUGH.**

My sandwich flies everywhere and all the girls go,

"EEEwwwwwwwwwwwww, TOM!"

It's really embarrassing.

There are bits of slightly chewed sandwich on the floor and table around me that I attempt to pick up.

"Sorry – it went down the wrong way," I try to explain.

Amy's mum asks me if I'm OK or need a glass of water.

"No, thanks. I'm just not that hungry any more."

It's not much of an excuse but I hope I don't have to eat another TUNA SANDWICH.

"You've got food in your hair," AMY tells Florence - so I say

sorry again.

AMY, Florence and Indrani carry on eating while I sit there watching and feeling awkward.

"Are you SURE you don't want anything else, Tom?" AMY's mum asks me.

"Nothing for me thanks - I'm fine.
I really don't want anything at all, honestly.
I'm just not that hungry. So don't worry about me.
I can't eat anything else - AT ALL. I couldn't eat another thing - really." (That should do it.)
I've made SUCH a big deal about NOT wanting ANYTHING else to eat that there's no going back when Amy's mum brings out ...

I made a mistake.

CAKE...

"Are you SURE you don't want some cake?" AMY asks me.

"No ... nothing else thanks," I say in a slightly  high-pitched voice. I just sit there and watch them eat CAKE.

My tummy starts RUMBLING so I do a sort of humming noise to try and cover it up.

Hmmmmmmm

Rumble

Rumble

"Is that you humming?" AMY asks me in-between mouthfuls of cake.

"Yes, don't worry about me. My dad will be here soon." (I hope he will be.)

Then I start hummmmming a **DOGZOMBIES** tune.  All the girls look at me again.

"It's one of the songs we play in the band. You know the band I'm in, **DOGZOMBIES**?" I explain.

"Yes, Tom – we know your band," **AMY** says.

"We're working on LOADS of new tunes. We're going to be the BEST BAND in the world," I tell them excitedly

(trying not to think about cake).

"How are you going to do that?" Florence asks me.

"We're working on a PLAN."

I'm hoping they won't ask me what our PLAN is as I can't remember.

"What's the PLAN then?" Indrani wonders.

"Must be a good one," Florence adds.

(Why did I say anything?)

I'm **VERY** happy when the doorbell goes. **Ding**

Dong

"**OH** ... never mind. I'll have to tell you all about it another time." (Phew.)

My dad's arrived " " and he's explaining to Amy's mum (she's called Brenda, I find out),

"I've been at the LEAFY GREEN OLD FOLKS' HOME, Brenda. My parents were visiting friends when the whole place had a **POWER CUT!** SO they called me and asked if I could come in and help out. Vera got stuck under the hairdryer and they all had to have an emergency COLD lunch."

I'm stuck.

"Sounds DRAMATIC!"

"**W**ell - the worst thing was I left my PHONE at home, so I missed all the calls from school and Rita. But I'm here now!" Dad explains. Then he SPOTS the chocolate cake.

"Looking at that **CAKE** I'm sure Tom's been fine!"

"Tom didn't want any – did you, Tom?" **AMY** tells him.

Dad does a sort of **CARTOON** double take and looks **SHOCKED**. Which is a bit over the TOP.

"REALLY? Tom didn't have any CAKE. Are you feeling all right?"

"Dad!" I sigh.

I just want Dad to be q u i e t so we can leave, but he won't stop chatting. Now he's telling them all about our holiday – what we ate (?), the BAD weather.

I'm thinking...

PLEASE don't mention BIN LINERS, Dad... Please.

"Tom's mum made him a RAIN CAPE out of a BIN LINER. It worked though, didn't it, Tom?"

"No one's interested, Dad – we should go," I sigh.

"I am – you WORE a bin liner? Did it work?" Florence wants to know.

"What did it look like?" Indrani adds.

"I SAW it. It looked like a bin liner that was a cape. It had a HOOD and everything!"

(I forgot AMY was there on the holiday – great.)
"I need to feed **Marble** now really," I say and get ready to go.

"What do you say, Tom?" Dad says.

"NOW," I add.

Dad glares at me. "Manners?"

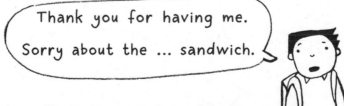

Thank you for having me. Sorry about the ... sandwich.

(I can't wait to get home.)

As we walk back, I have to tell Dad how I AVOIDED the tuna sandwiches.

"You shouldn't be SO FUSSY!" Dad LAUGHS. He seems to be in a good mood considering the power cut and everything. I'm not LAUGHING about the CAKE though.

"Not eating cake must have been HARD."

"It was tough."

Someone coming!

The first thing I do when I get home is check **Marble's** OK. Even with the noise of the STORM, he's still FAST asleep. It doesn't look like he's moved AT all. zzzzzzzzzzzzzz

I hope **Marble** isn't saving all his energy for night-time.

As Marble's not awake I could try doing my **MYSTERY STORY** homework. Mr Fullerman would be VERY impressed if I brought that in. Trouble is, I can't think of ANYTHING to write about. Nothing comes to mind... Maybe I could write about **Marble.** Or...

I could do a doodle instead. I'm quite tired so even if **Marble** does wake up, I'll probably just sleep through any of his NOISE.

Or maybe not.

I'm so tired after another night of **Marble's** activity that I get confused and brush my teeth before breakfast. I don't want to tell Mum or Dad (and especially not Delia) that **Marble's** been keeping me awake, AND is trickier to look after than I expected.

I practise my "**I'**m WIDE AWAKE AND NOT SLEEPY AT ALL!" face.

It's the best I can do.

"Morning! Are you OK?" Mum asks.

"Yes, thanks, I'm feeling GREAT -

LOOK HOW

GREAT I'm FEELING!"

"**Y**ou look **WEIRD** - sit down," Delia says.

"How's **Marble?** Still in his cage, I hope?"
Dad asks me.

"Of course. He does all these FUNNY things.
I LOVE it!
It's BRILLIANT having a **pet.**"

"Make the most of it - he's NOT staying,"
Delia says.

I take no notice of her and put some
bread in the toaster.

"I thought I heard **Marble's** wheel
SQUEAKING last night," Dad tells me.
I say nothing. "It was very loud. I'm surprised
it didn't wake you up, Tom," he adds.

"I didn't hear anything," I say as the toast pops up
and I put some butter on it.

$\mathbb{D}$ad says he might take a look at it. (Secretly I'm VERY PLEASED. ☺) I carry on eating my toast. I rest my hand on my face and chew slowly. The movement makes my head go up and down and makes me feel a bit

SLEEPY...

Then Mum starts talking about family stuff and that's when I really switch Off. I only close my eyes for a few seconds and my face falls forward into my toast.

Huh?

It doesn't stop me eating it though.

Delia looks at me and says,

"That's GROSS."

Then she does a MASSIVE SNEEZE.

"No, THAT'S GROSS,"

I repeat as she goes to get a tissue. I'm lucky Mum and Dad missed my head slip because now they're talking about work stuff. Dad's excited because he's just got a NEW JOB.

"I'm doing the posters and album cover

for the PLASTIC CUP reunion. ⟶

I have lots of ideas already – and I'm meeting the band tonight, which should be interesting."

"That's one way of putting it," Mum LAUGHs.

All this talk of bands reminds me that we have to make a PLAN for our DOGZOMBIES video.

I'll have a chat with Norman and Derek today in school, because right now...

... I'm imagining **DOGZOMBIES**

ARE the BEST BAND IN THE WHOLE

WORLD,

with an endless supply of SNACKS given to us

at every gig and band practice. Like this.

I'm so busy thinking about our band that when Dad offers me a lift to school, I don't hear him. (AT FIRST.)

"**TOM!** Would you like a lift into school this morning? You'll be quite early as I have to leave NOW, though."

It sounds like a good idea – especially as I'm a bit tired. AND it would be nice to sit in the CAR. BUT then I remember the **SHAKE and WAKE!** kids. Hmmmm... I don't want to bump into them again.

"I'm fine, Dad – I'll walk in with Derek,"

I tell him. (It's for the best.)

Not walking on the pavement cracks slows us down on the way to school SO MUCH that Norman catches up and joins in. We have LOADS of time to chat about our **DOGZOMBIES** video.

"Let's use my dad's camera phone,"

I suggest.

"We should make it BRILLIANT!"

Norman adds. (That's sorted then.)

Over the next few days we TALK about our music video PLAN a LOT. There are loads of important things to discuss, like:

Eventually we decide to film our video at my house at the weekend on my dad's phone and sing our new song, "**DOGZOMBIES** RULE" (and wear shades).

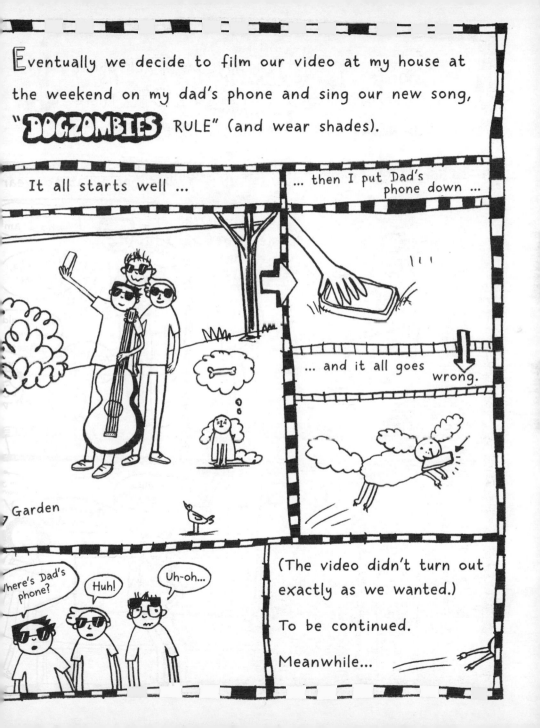

It all starts well ...

... then I put Dad's phone down ...

... and it all goes wrong.

Garden

Where's Dad's phone?

Huh!

Uh-oh...

(The video didn't turn out exactly as we wanted.)

To be continued.

Meanwhile...

Sunday Lunch with the cousins

I honestly thought that things couldn't get any worse (after trying to make our music video).

I manage to get SOME sleep before **Marble** really goes for it on his wheel, which starts SQUEAKING again.

SQUEAK

SQUEAK

To block out the light, I put on Delia's sunglasses and wear a woolly hat that muffles the sound.

It works for a bit – but isn't very comfortable.

BIFF BOFF BIFF BOFF BIFF

So I decide I might as well get up early again. We're going to the cousins' for lunch today – which I'm not entirely looking forward to. 🙁

As soon as I'm awake, (sort of) **Marble** goes off to sleep. I get dressed and go downstairs. Dad's already up and Mum's there too. Dad picks up his keys to go out and straight away she says, "Where are you off to so early, Frank?"

Dad holds up his phone.

"It had an accident. I'm going to try and get it fixed."

(I keep quiet.)

"Don't forget we're going for LUNCH. Please don't be late back. We need to make an EFFORT," Mum tells him.

"Eating Kevin's  roast potatoes is always an EFFORT." Dad LAUGHs while pretending to bite on something TOUGH.

Mum doesn't laugh, but I still think it's **FUNNY**.  Ha! Ha! Then Delia comes down and she's on her way OUT too.

"Where are you going?" Mum wants to know.

"To meet **Avril**."

"You haven't forgotten about Sunday lunch have you?" Mum asks.

"What Sunday lunch?"
Delia says.

"I told you about it ages ago!" Mum says, panicking.

"I'm joking. **CHILL**, I'll meet you there." Mum **HATES** being told to **CHILL**, so Delia says it a **lot**.

"Don't be late!" Mum tells her as she leaves.

As I'm eating breakfast, I'm thinking it would be good to go over to Derek's and work out another video plan. I get up and ask Mum,
"Can I go to Derek's?"

"What for?" Mum wants to know.

"We have very important **DOGZOMBIES** stuff to chat about," I explain.

"OK – I'll come and get you at midday. And NO SNACKING – remember we're having lunch!" Mum reminds me.

(As if I'd forget.)

I couldn't have picked a better time to arrive. ☺

"Hi, Tom. We're having Pancakes.

Do you want some?" Derek asks me.

"What do YOU think?" Working on a NEW

DOGZOMBIES video kind of gets put to one

side when there's PANCAKES to be eaten!

Mr and Mrs Fingle have made a ton of them too.

I can hardly WAIT!

They've even got CHOCOLATE sauce.

Choco Sauce

Mrs Fingle says, "I hope you're hungry, Tom!"

"YES, I am!"

I help myself to THREE **massive** pancakes and they're delicious.

Mmmm
Mmmm
Mmmm

As we're all tucking in Mr Fingle tells us how the **PLASTIC CUP** reunion is going. "Not well, I'm afraid. There's been some 'musical differences' but I'm still looking forward to their first gig."

Grrrr

Derek says, "We always agree on songs, don't we?"

I nod as my mouth is full.

"I heard Rooster wasn't very helpful with your music video," Mrs Fingle says.

"You can say THAT again," Derek sighs. (Rooster is in the garden safely away from the pancakes.)

"Dad's getting his phone fixed so we can try again," I suggest between mouthfuls.

"Great!" Derek says and we both add more chocolate sauce.

I've eaten SO many pancakes that I have to undo the top button on my trousers.

OOOFFF Then Derek asks if I want to try the TOFFEE SAUCE.

"I LOVE TOFFEE SAUCE!" I say, and I pour some over another bit of pancake

Mmmm Mmmm and finish it ALL UP.

"I'm STUFFED!" I tell Derek.

Ohhhhhhh...

FULL

FULL

"Me too. Let's go and lie on the sofa," he suggests. (It's a good idea.)

Glancing up at the clock I realize it's nearly MIDDAY and Mum said she was coming to collect me then. We haven't had the chance to talk about our VIDEO – but the pancakes were ACE. ☺

Mum arrives on time so I ease off the sofa and tell Derek, "Don't mention the pancakes."

OK.

Mrs Fingle and Mum are chatting by the door when she asks,

"Are you doing anything nice later?"

"Not really, no," I say.

"That's not true, Tom! We're having a BIG Sunday lunch with the family!"

"GOSH – I hope you're still hungry!" Mrs Fingle LAUGHs.

"Always!" I say, hoping Mum didn't notice that. I wave BYE to Derek and say, "Thank you for having me – and all the other stuff too."

(I'm careful not to mention pancakes.)

Mum tells me to get straight in the car.
"Did you have anything to eat, Tom?"
she wants to know.

"Not really," I say without going into too much
detail. "You've got chocolate sauce on your
face," she says, and passes me a tissue.

(Whoops.)

I wipe it off quickly and undo ANOTHER button
to make my tummy feel more comfortable.
It's a relief to sit down again – I'm so full.

"Where's Delia?" Dad wants to know as he gets in
the car.

"She's meeting us there," Mum tells him.

"Are you sure she'll turn up?"

"No..." Mum sighs, then adds, "You know what Aunty Alice is like if people don't eat her food, Tom."

"You'd think she'd be used to that by now,"  Dad says, LAUGHING.

"Please don't say things like that when we're there, Frank. And, Tom – you'd better not have eaten too many snacks at Derek's."

(I say nothing.)

"All I want is a nice lunch with everyone getting on together as a family. How difficult can that be?" Mum asks us.

VERY, Dad says.

"Aren't we supposed to BRING something with us?" he adds.

"I FORGOT the pudding! WHY didn't you remind me?" Mum shouts.

"I just DID," Dad says, turning the car round to go home.

 All this speeding around isn't helping my STOMACH at all. (I've run out of buttons to undo on my trousers.)

We pull up outside the house and Mum runs inside and back out again really *FAST*. "We'll be LATE now, and your brother will make a comment about us NOT being on time," she sighs.

"Probably," Dad agrees.
Whenever we go over to Uncle Kevin and Aunty Alice's house, Mum and Dad always have a discussion about things we're NOT meant to talk about.

(Today is no different.)

"**D**on't mention the holiday and staying in the wrong villa will you?" Mum says.

"Or about you climbing in through the window, Tom!" Dad adds as he swerves round a corner.

"**FRANK, SLOW DOWN!**" Mum tells Dad, but it's too late. There's a **BIG** blob of mousse on her lap now. SPLAT

(Mum's not happy.)

Great... "Do you want to go back home and get changed?" Dad asks, trying to be helpful.

"No, just try not to STOP-START so much," Mum sighs.

"I could stop and get some extra ice cream if you want?"

"**YES, please!**" I say from the back, even though I am full. (I always find room for extra ice cream.)

"Let's just get there, shall we?" Mum says.

(That's a "no" to ice cream, then.)

"You're here ... at LAST!"
Aunty Alice says as she
opens the door.
"Yes – sorry we're late,"
Mum says.
"That's OK – Delia and her
FRIEND are early."

"Delia's EARLY – with Avril?" Mum repeats.

(Not Avril again.)

"Yes – luckily we have plenty of food," Aunty Alice

tells us. (Not that I'm hungry.)

We all go inside and Mum explains the stain on

her dress. "Sorry about the pudding. Frank's

driving didn't help."

"Driving's never been your strong point, has it,

Frank?" is the first thing that Uncle Kevin says.

"Lovely to see you too, Kevin. The apron

suits you." Dad smiles and follows

him into the kitchen.

Uncle Kevin takes the pudding from Aunty Alice and puts it to one side.

"You REALLY shouldn't have bothered, Rita, we have a delicious pudding already," he smiles.

"Well I did - so there it is," Mum sighs. Then Uncle Kevin RUFFLES my hair (which is annoying - but I keep quiet). My cousins are watching so I say, "Hi." I think they've grown taller since I last saw them, or that's what it FEELS like standing next to them.

The first thing they say to me is, "Tom, come upstairs - we have something for you." My cousins like to play TRICKS on me, so the last thing I'm expecting to see is ...

... a BIG bowl of **jelly beans.**

(I'm _still_ suspicious though.)

Maybe they're all disgusting flavours – OR they've licked them. Just in case, I say, "Yum, **jelly beans** – after YOU," and let them go first.

"If you insist." The cousins take a big handful each and `POP` them in their mouths, so I'm guessing they're OK.

I eat a few now and put the rest in my pocket for later. I've still got the buttons on my trousers undone, which feels a lot more comfortable, but the WEIGHT of all the **jelly beans** starts pulling them down. So I eat a few more just to be on the safe side.

Mum spots me chewing.

"I hope you're not spoiling your appetite, Tom."

"Mmmmmm, no,"

I manage to say with my mouth FULL.

Everyone heads down to the kitchen where my dad asks the cousins, "How's your band doing, lads?"

"It's not our band any more – it's Dad's band really."

"Taking over things? That doesn't sound like your dad!" he LAUGHS.

Uncle Kevin stops carving the chicken to say, "HANG ON A SECOND ...

that's not quite right. LET me explain!"

(The cousins sigh.)

"The boys dropped out of the band, so a few of the other parents and I thought it would be FUN to keep it going. It's not like we're planning to do any GIGS," he LAUGHS.

Ha!
Ha!

"**B**ut you said you WANTED to play a gig, Dad," the cousins remind him **LOUDLY.**

"Did I? I don't remember saying that. Who'd come and listen to us lot playing anyway?"

" "**I WOULD!**" I say.

"Me too!" Dad says, nudging me.

"They play **RuBBISH** songs though," the cousins warn us – which sets off a **BIG** discussion about which songs they think are BAD and which are GOOD.

Who are the Beatles?

You're kidding...

They're joking.

Beyoncé.

Elvis is king!

If **A**unty **A**lice hadn't stepped in to tell us that Granny and Granddad had arrived, it would STILL be going on...

Aunty Alice tells us all to go and help ourselves to lunch, which is EXCELLENT news for me, because I'm not very hungry. It means I can do that thing of SPREADING my food out across my plate to make it look all nice and FULL. (No one will guess I've already eaten ~~2~~ ~~3~~ ~~4~~ some pancakes with a ~~little~~ LOT of toffee and chocolate sauce.)

We're here!

There – mission accomplished.

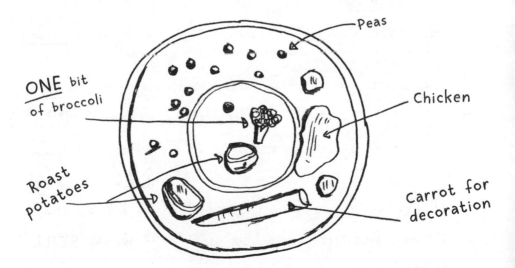

Peas

ONE bit of broccoli

Chicken

Roast potatoes

Carrot for decoration

Granny and Granddad are explaining what happened at the LEAFY GREEN OLD FOLKS' HOME after the POWER CUT and why they're late.

"We took a dish of macaroni cheese and grapes over as their ovens still aren't working properly thanks to the power cut."

"I drove through a lot of puddles!" Granddad adds.

"I made it for our dinner but they need the food more than we do," Granny says.

Lucky escape, the cousins whisper.

Then Granny carries on chatting.

"Poor Vera's not happy at all – her heated rollers are broken and her hair's gone as FLAT as a pancake!"

The word "pancake" reminds me of how **full** I still am.

Vera before power cut

Vera after power cut

No one's noticed my s p a c e d o u t food. So
I shouldn't have to eat too much.

Then Uncle Kevin only goes and says,

"You've hardly got ANYTHING to eat, Tom!
Have some more chicken and roast potatoes."

PLONK!

He puts LOADS more
on my PLATE!

Mum doesn't think I've got enough
GREEN vegetables either, so she puts

some on as well. I have NO idea how I'm going to

eat it ALL now. Sigh...

Delia and Avril come and sit down and
they've only got vegetables on their
plates. (They could have had mine.)

"Would you like some chicken to go with that?"
Uncle Kevin asks them.

 "No thanks – we're both VEGETARIAN."

"Since WHEN have you been vegetarian?"
Mum wonders, looking **Surprised.**

 "Since this morning. But we've been
thinking about it for a long time,"
Delia adds while Avril agrees by nodding.
With everyone sitting round the table, Uncle Kevin
taps his spoon on the side of his glass and says,
"Before we start I'd like to say a FEW WORDS."

"How FEW? We're all hungry!" Dad says.
(Not everyone is.)

Uncle Kevin ignores his comment
and carries on with his (SPEECH.)
He thanks everyone for coming and
says how delicious everything looks.

While all this chat is going on, I loosen my
trousers a tiny bit more to make room for LUNCH.

Sigh...

But then **U**ncle **K**evin says,

"Let's raise our glasses to
FAMILY... Oh, and friends too, Avril."

Everyone STANDS to CLINK their glasses together

but as I get UP⬆

my trousers start

FALLING DOWN...

If the cousins hadn't started SHOUTING,

"TOM'S TROUSERS!
TOM'S TROUSERS!"

no one would have noticed. I have to —dive

under the table and pretend I've dropped a fork.

"Fine ... just dropped a FORK," I say, doing up a few buttons. The cousins are still LAUGHING when I sit back down.

"Do you need a clean fork, Tom?" Aunty Alice asks me. "Can one of you get a fork please?" she says to the cousins.

It takes TWO of them to bring me a tiny BABY fork. "That's all we could find," they say. (I'm not entirely convinced.) But eating lunch with it will take even longer – which suits me fine.

While I'm trying to scoop up one pea at a time, I listen to the conversation Uncle Kevin is having with Delia and Avril.

I could have told him not to bother...

"So, Avril – what are you up to at the moment?"

"Eating..."

"I mean ... are you studying?"

"Yes..."

"Are you studying anything interesting?"

"Sometimes."

"Do you have a FAVOURITE subject?"

"No..."

(And so it goes on.... Ha! Ha!)

The cousins are asking Delia questions too, which I have to admit she's quite good at answering.

"Why do you wear sunglasses all the time, Delia?"

"So I don't have to look at kids like YOU too closely."

"What's your favourite colour?"

"PINK."

"Really?"

"What do you think?"

"No."

"You two don't miss a thing."

The "misheard lyrics" chat gives me the chance to tell everyone about the song I sang in assembly.

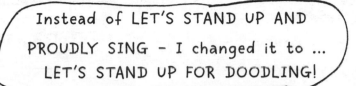

Instead of LET'S STAND UP AND PROUDLY SING - I changed it to ... LET'S STAND UP FOR DOODLING!

(The cousins laugh - Mum doesn't.)

I didn't get into ANY trouble at all.

Granddad goes BACK to talking about music videos - or, as he calls them, POP videos.

CLICK

CLICK

)),

CLICK

I'd like to be in one of THOSE. I could play the SPOONS!

Then he does a demonstration of his spoon skills

(which is very impressive).

Delia tells him he COULD be in a video if he wants.

"There are LOADS of videos of old people recording their OWN versions of famous songs online."

(Which is news to me.)

Granny sounds interested. [What fun!]

The cousins tell us about one they've seen already...

"The old folks dress up and sing the Beastie Boys, 'Fight For Your Right to PARTY', AND they're ALL about 150 years OLD!"

"Younger than us then!" Granddad says, winking at Granny.

"A SLIGHT exaggeration!" Uncle Kevin points out.

"There's hope for all of US!" Dad LAUGHs.

Granny seems VERY keen on the video idea - but not as KEEN as Granddad! [We should make our own pop video!]

[What a good idea! There's a NEW resident at the LEAFY GREEN HOME who has a VERY good singing voice. Apparently he used to be a BIG country-and-western STAR in his DAY.]

"What's the new resident's name?" Mum wonders.

He doesn't talk very much - but I think he's called Tony. His band was
Teacup Tony and the Saucers!

"I've heard of them! That's a great name for a band, isn't it?" Dad says.

LIKE **DOGZOMBIES**!
We made a video for our band!

I add enthusiastically.

How exciting! Can we see it? Granny asks.

"No, it got ruined - we have to make a NEW one now. If Dad lets me."

"Only if you keep Rooster away!" Dad says.

"What happened?" Granny asks.

So I tell EVERYONE about my

MUSIC VIDEO DISASTER...

I made a SPECTACULAR sign for the start of the video.

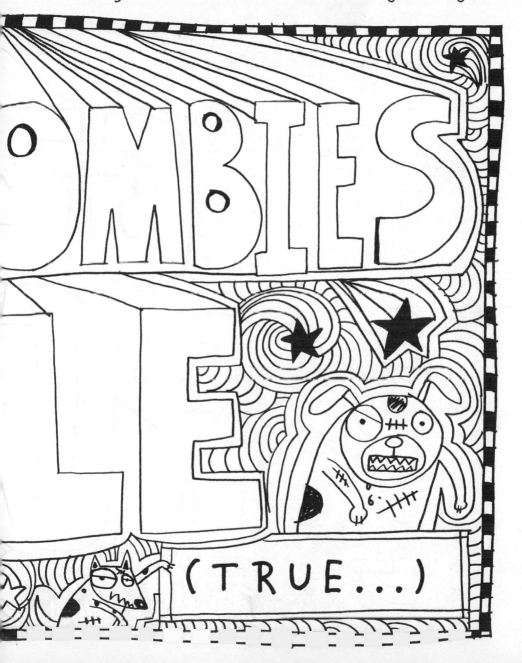

(TRUE...)

DOGZOMBIES VIDEO

(The making of)

After school, me, **D**erek and **N**orman finally got together to make a new video for the song "**DOGZOMBIES** RULE". Dad let us use his phone to film it on.

"Look after it, won't you?" he told me.

"Of COURSE I will," I said.

Rooster jumped over the fence to join us. We let him stay because we thought it was a good idea to have him "APPEAR" in the video (as he's a DOG – and we're called **DOGZOMBIES**).

Then we worked out where to stand (which took a while) and decided the garden was the best place to film. After practising some excellent ROCK-STAR POSES, we were ready to start.

Norman pogoing

We took turns filming each other singing and playing our song. Balancing the phone on the wall meant we could be in the same SHOT together while we sung the CHORUS of "**DOGZOMBIES** RULE".

Rooster got very excited and kept running in and out of our video. But we STILL managed to get it ALL filmed. After taking ONE last photo, I put the phone down while we did a high five to celebrate. And THAT'S

Stone

when Rooster decided to do some filming of his own.

He grabbed the phone in his MOUTH and RAN OFF. Derek shouted, "ROOSTER! DROP THAT PHONE! DROP IT RIGHT NOW!"

(Being a good dog ... he did.)

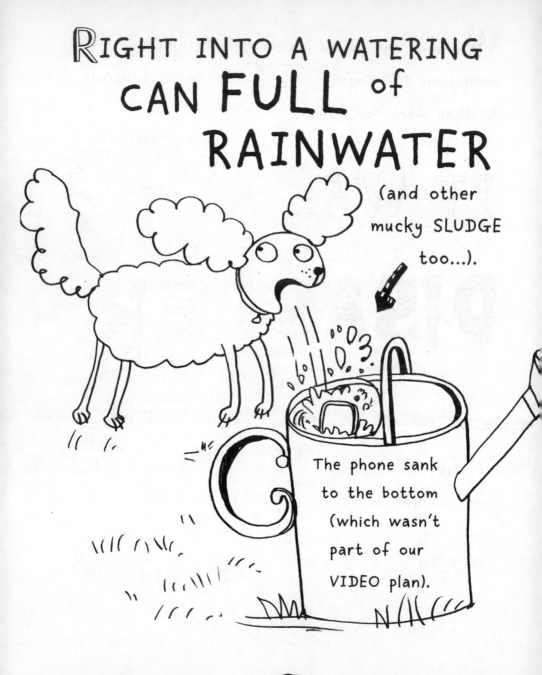

RIGHT INTO A WATERING CAN FULL of RAINWATER

(and other mucky SLUDGE too...).

The phone sank to the bottom (which wasn't part of our VIDEO plan).

We took the phone out – but it wouldn't even turn ON. The **WHOLE** VIDEO was GONE. All that work for nothing.

IT WAS A

DISASTER.

(Dad wasn't very pleased either.)

WE still want to make ANOTHER video. But this time Rooster won't be in it.

Woof!

Dad says, "To be FAIR, Tom, it wasn't a complete **DISASTER**. I took the phone to be fixed this morning and they gave me a NEW ONE instead. I got an UPGRADE too! LOOK!" Dad seems quite pleased with his fancy new phone, so that's something.

Then Granny makes a suggestion.

"We're having a FUNDRAISING bingo night to raise money for some of the electrical things that need replacing at LEAFY GREEN. Your band could come and play if you want, Tom?"

"How about Kevin's NEW band? This could be their first gig!" Mum suddenly suggests. Which is a MUCH better idea. The cousins start cheering.

Yes! Do it!

Uncle Kevin's not so sure.

Calm down, everyone.

"You might raise more money for them NOT to play!" Dad jokes.

"ACTUALLY, we're getting quite good!

But we still don't have a proper name yet," Uncle Kevin tells us. Immediately we start thinking of BAND NAMES for him.

Even Avril joins in!

The Wrinklies?

The Mid-Life Crisis Crew?

The Sell-By Dates?

The Overripes?

The Not-Bad Band?

The "It Was Our Band But Not Any More"?

You lot are HILARIOUS...

(I'm not sure he's going to use any of our suggestions.) Granny Mavis asks if anyone could help out and be the BINGO caller.

"Frank will do it – won't you?" Mum says before Dad can answer.

He says,

I'd love to...

(Like he has a choice now.)

The GOOD thing about all the CHATTER is it has helped me AVOID eating my lunch. I've nibbled a bit but most of it is STILL there. I'm trying to work out what to do when I SPOT the window open behind me – which gets me THINKING...

I could *LEAN* over and drop some of my food OUT of the window...

Easy.

It's worth a try. I'll just have to wait for the

RIGHT moment to do it.

Especially as my cousins seem to SPOT everything with their ...

EAGLE EYES.

T HAT **moment** arrives sooner than I expect.

Granddad **BITES** down into a very crispy
roast potato which makes his TEETH
SPRING right OUT of his
mouth and land on
Avril's plate.

At first she doesn't notice.
It's when Avril puts down
her glass that she gets a
SURPRISE.

HUH?

The cousins start LAUGHING
and do silly voices saying,
"'ELLO, Avril! 'ELLO, Avril! 'ELLO, Avril!" like the
teeth are speaking to her.

For someone who doesn't say very much, Avril can
scream REALLY loudly!

AGGHHHHHHHHHH!

Aunty Alice tries to cover the teeth up by throwing a napkin on to the plate, only she MISSES completely and it goes right into Uncle Kevin's face. While all this is going on I grab a handful of food and **LEAN** back casually towards the OPEN window. Then I drop it out as fast as I can. I have enough time for a few more handfuls before everything calms down.

"*Thowwy* about THAT," Granddad says as he picks up his teeth. Delia has taken **Avril** to the kitchen. She comes back in to tell us, "**Avril's** been traumatized by TEETH – so we're both going home."

Aunty Alice offers to give Delia and **Avril** some pudding to take with them (which is NOT really deserved if you ask me).

I'm not worried WHAT happens now because I have an EMPTY plate (nearly) which is a result.

I'm ALMOST tempted to have some pudding myself. (I've got a tiny bit of room...)

Mum and Dad take the plates into the kitchen (including MINE) while Uncle Kevin brings in a fancy cake with fruit and all sorts of things – AND some ice cream too.

Mum adds her chocolate mousse to the table as well.

Nearly forgot, Uncle Kevin says. (He didn't.)

Mum says it's a SHAME Delia and Avril have left.

"More pudding for us!" Dad LAUGHS, and Mum gives him a LOOK.

As Aunty Alice starts to dish out the cake, Mum looks up and says,

"I didn't know you had CATS."

Aunty Alice says, "We don't."

"**W**hat's that cat doing on the window then?" Mum asks.

Uncle **K**evin tries to *SHOOOO* it away, then *leans* out of the window to check if it's gone.

"THERE ARE CATS EVERYWHERE!"

he says (and not in a good way). Uh-oh.

The cousins make EVERYTHING WORSE by **SHOUTING,**

"CATS! CATS! CATS. Tom – CATS! Let's go!"

like they've never seen a CAT before. Then they rush outside and drag me with them. I'm HOPING by the time we get there, the cats will all be gone.

But they're not...

AND there's FOOD (my food) everywhere.
I try to get rid of some of the EVIDENCE by
kicking it into the bushes, but I just make it LOOK
WORSE. It's like a CRIME scene and I've been
CAUGHT red-handed.

Everyone is STARING at me, wondering WHAT'S
going on. I do my best to look BAFFLED. Here's my

"HOW DID **THIS** HAPPEN?" face:

I keep saying "I WONDER what happened?" and I "SHAKE" my head in the hope that no one will suspect that it was ME. (Not guilty ... much.)

Uncle Kevin asks us all to go back to the house while Aunty Alice keeps trying to shoo the cats away. Which would be a lot easier to do –

if the cousins weren't stroking and feeding them.

I leave them to it and decide to stay in the background and [not] make a FUSS.

I'm hoping that no one will put two and two together and work out how the food got outside.

After everything that's gone on, I decide NOT to have any pudding. It's for the best.

← Mum's wobbly chocolate mousse

THE FOSSILS say we're ALL invited to the
LEAFY GREEN fundraising event.
"I'd LOVE a copy of your new song, Tom!"
Granny Mavis tells me.
"I'll sort that one on my NEW phone!
I've still got a recording of the music,"
Dad says, which is something.

No one says anything more about the cats.
So I start to wonder if MAYBE I might have got away with dropping my food out of the window after all? ☺ I keep on thinking that right up until the car journey home.

"So, TOM, why did you throw your food out of the window?" Dad asks me.

"WHAT? Me... Errrrrrrrrr..."

I do a lot of EEEErrrrrrrring, but I can't think of a good excuse so I tell them about the pancakes at Derek's.

"You had FOUR pancakes!" Mum says, surprised.

"And TWO sauces. They were delicious."

Yum!

Surprisingly Mum and Dad don't seem THAT angry about it. But Mum says I HAVE to write a "sorry" note.

Do I HAVE to?

Yes!

YES!

(It could be worse, I suppose.)

When we get home Mum gives me some paper to write my SORRY card on.

"Do it after you've looked after **Marble,**" she reminds me.

(I have a lot of things to get done now.)

I take all the paper upstairs, then clean out **Marble's** cage, making sure he doesn't RUN OFF. So far he's hardly moved at all.

Weee!

ROCK WEEKLY

With **Marble** back asleep, after a quick read of my comics and a **ROCK WEEKLY,** I start making the SORRY card. 😟

What should I say? First I draw a **MONSTER** saying sorry. But I'm not sure that will be enough.

Sorry.

So I add ...

a CAT ...

Sorry.

... and another holding a chicken leg.

(Maybe not.)

I have another think and write this instead...

Dear

Aunty Alice and Uncle Kevin,

I didn't **think** it was possible to

LIKE ➡ a lunch as ᴹmuch as I did,

your food was DELICIOUS. ☺

It tasted *REALLY* YUMMY. I was

☹ **SAD** I couldn't eat it **ALL**

(sorry) I really tried. I was **FULL.**

Love

Tom X X

PS The cats loved
the chicken.
Sorry again.

Then I have the EXTRA idea to ADD a very special PAPER CHAIN into the envelope. (Nothing says "I'm sorry" like a paper-chain **MONSTER**.)* I have lots of spare sheets to use so I grab some and start CUTTING them into the right shape to draw on.

Folds

Cut here

Dear

My table's a bit messy but once it's done I POP it in the envelope with my note.

*See pages 226-227 for "How to Make a Paper-Chain Monster"

Mum's already written their address on the envelope AND put a stamp on it, so I stick it down and give it back to her. She looks very pleased with me.
I EVEN clean my desk and THROW AWAY all the scraps of paper too.

I AM OFFICIALLY THE

BEST CHILD

in the WHOLE FAMILY,

which isn't that hard.

I don't think.

And when I get ready for bed I discover some

jelly beans in my pocket from earlier ...

Hooray! →

... which is a  and puts me in a REALLY good mood. I don't mind that I'm going to bed a bit early either.

I'll just get MORE sleep,

which will be VERY nice.

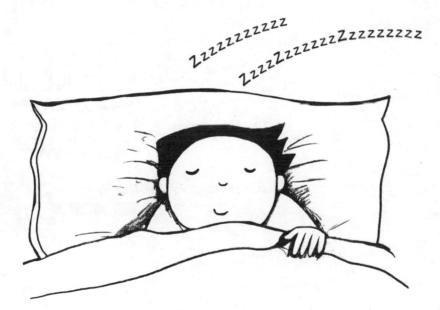

BOFF BIFF

BOFF

BIFF

BOFF ...

Mark's coming to pick
Marble up tomorrow.

(Phew...)

I was hoping that the POWER CUT
would stop me from going to school for a bit.

(No such luck. 😞)

"School's open again. No day off for you, Tom,"
Dad tells me.

Here's my "I'M TIRED AND NOT
LOOKING FORWARD TO LESSONS" face.

(Groan.)

When I go and call for Derek he looks at me and
says, "Whooa, YOU look sleepy."

"Is this better?" I ask.

"Kind of,"
Derek says, not really convinced.

I do my <u>best</u> to perk up as I tell him that Mark's
coming to pick **Marble** up today.

"I'll miss him, BUT I miss SLEEPING more."

(True.)

At school everything seems like it's back to normal – until Derek points out a SIGN hanging up. "That came around quickly," he sighs. – Sigh

Today turns out to be the FIRST time we're doing

SHAKE and WAKE!

"Let's go to our bench for a rest – we might need it," I suggest.

As soon as we sit down, the kids from 2D come and join us.

"Don't worry, we're moving," I say before they can ask.

But it's not long before the rest of the school and the teachers gather round as well.

"Are you ready for **SHAKE and WAKE!?**"

Mr Keen asks us all.

(Not really.)

So exciting! Morning, all!

Yeah!

Ready

The music starts blaring out of the new speakers and the kids from 2D leap into action. There's NO WAY to get out of this. I just have to join in – like everyone else.

Here goes...

"Did you enjoy THAT?"

Mr Keen asks us at the end.

Red face

Most of the school says, "YES!"

I'm too puffed out to speak.

He says thank you to class 2D kids and

we give them a round of applause.

"They've all set the bar VERY high.
NEXT week we'll have a different
class to teach us a NEW
SHAKE and WAKE!!"

Mr Keen is VERY enthusiastic.

"Brilliant," I say to Derek

who looks surprised.

"I'm joking," I tell him.

All I want to do now is go and sit down and RELAX.
I'm glad **SHAKE and WAKE!** is all finished.
It could have been worse I suppose, and the most
awkward part of the day is OVER...

"Tom, do you have your MYSTERY STORY homework for me?"

is the first thing Mr Fullerman asks.

(I spoke too soon.)

He gives me the morning to do it in class. At least

I'm not the only one writing their story. (Brad

Galloway and Amber are doing it too.) The trouble

is I can't think of ANYTHING to write about.

My mind has gone blank.

Then Marcus does that stupid

snake thing ... so I write this...

IT'S A MYSTERY?

by Tom Gates

When a big, strange **BLOB** appeared in the

park, it was a **MYSTERY** what it was.

It just sat there doing nothing.

All the children were told NOT to go

near it in case it was DANGEROUS. But there was

one boy – called **Sucram*** (see what I did?) who

thought he knew best and took no notice at all.

He decided it would be **FUN** to ANNOY the

BLOB by poking it with a stick.

Then he WOBBLED it with his hand,

and did stupid SNAKE arms at it too.

"SEE? This **BLOB** is NOT dangerous at all.

It's just a **BLOB** that does

NOTHING," Sucram shouted

and hissed at it.

(Sucram was a very annoying boy.)

The BLOB suddenly started to get BIGGER

and BIGGER and BIGGER.

Then it opened its mouth...

* MARCUS backwards

179

It was a complete **MYSTERY** whatever happened to Sucram. (It wasn't.) The BLOB went back to having a quiet life and didn't bother anyone else at all.

The End.

(Mr Fullerman likes my story.)

Well done, Tom – I'm not sure I'd like to meet the Blob in the park! See what you can do when you concentrate.

After school

Derek and Norman are coming back to mine for a couple of reasons:

1: To say BYE to **Marble** as Mark is collecting him tonight.

2: To make plans for another music VIDEO.

(Both are very important.)

All the way home Norman is re-enacting the **SHAKE and WAKE!** dance. He's doing a LOT more shaking than I remember though.

"It's <u>OUR</u> class's turn next week," he tells us.

"Count me <u>OUT!</u>" I say straight away.

"Like you'll have a CHOICE!" Derek reminds me.

"No - but I could have a BAD LEG."

I point out, pretending to LIMP.

(It's my backup plan.)

I practise limping all the way home. (Just in case.)

The FIRST thing we do at my house is go and

check on **Marble,** who's asleep.

I get all his stuff together so he's ready

for when Mark picks him up.

"That's what he does **ALL** day,"

I tell Norman and Derek.

"Not much else. He gets lively at night though."

When Mark arrives to collect him he's still asleep.

"How was **Marble?**" Mark wants to know.

"He was brilliant - I LOVED having a pet.

IT was the BEST!" I say really loudly ...

... because I **K**NOW Mum is listening.
(I don't mention the noise or

sleepless nights, of course.)

I wave BYE to **Marble,** but he doesn't move as
he's still asleep. As usual.

Bye.

After Mark goes the three of us start chatting
about **DOGZOMBIES** and WHAT we're going to
do for another video.

"Keep Rooster away for a start,"
Derek LAUGHs.

"We can use my dad's NEW phone!"
I suggest. "I'm sure he won't mind."
(He might – but I'll work that out later.)
Then we do a quick practice of
"**DOGZOMBIES** Rule".

As we're congratulating ourselves, Mum suddenly
shouts from downstairs...

TOM GATES, WE NEED TO TALK!

Which doesn't sound very good.

I can hear her coming upstairs.

"I haven't done anything!"

I tell Norman and Derek.

When Mum comes in she looks really **cross.**

"I'm sorry, boys, but you'll have to GO home.
I need to talk to Tom."

"OK, see you at school,"
Norman says and Derek
gives me a look as they both leave.

I have NO idea what is going on or WHY I'm in trouble.

Then Mum says, "SO when I asked you to send
your aunty and uncle a note saying
sorry, which bit of that did
you **not** understand?"

"All of it... I mean **NONE** of it!"
(I got that wrong.)

"Well they weren't that happy to get THIS
from you, Tom. Honestly. What were you thinking?"

Mum shows me a note that's signed by me.

Dear

Aunty Alice

I didn't

LIKE

your food

It tasted

😞 SAD

(sorry)

Love

Tom X

Mum isn't in the mood to listen to me and says I'll have to send a "PROPER" note.

"BUT this time I'll be reading it BEFORE you post it to them."

"But I said nice things!"

"Early to bed for you tonight, I think."

Mum doesn't let me explain, which is VERY annoying as the other part of the note MUST be around somewhere!

I'm trying to think  WHAT could have happened to the note.

The only GOOD thing about being sent to bed EARLY is now **Marble's** not here, I'll get a WHOLE night's sleep. BUT the **BAD** thing about NOT having **Marble** is ...

Delia comes in to bother me.

I hear you're in trouble.

So you don't want this pizza?

"Go away, Delia," I sigh.

She won't give me any pizza unless I show her my NOTE. We do a swap and she thinks it's hilarious!

"It's only HALF the note," I try to explain.

"Don't worry, Tom. It's FUNNY," she tells me - ALMOST being NICE.

I get ready for bed and keep wondering WHAT happened to that note.

It takes me a while to go to sleep because I'm thinking too much. Eventually I drift off...

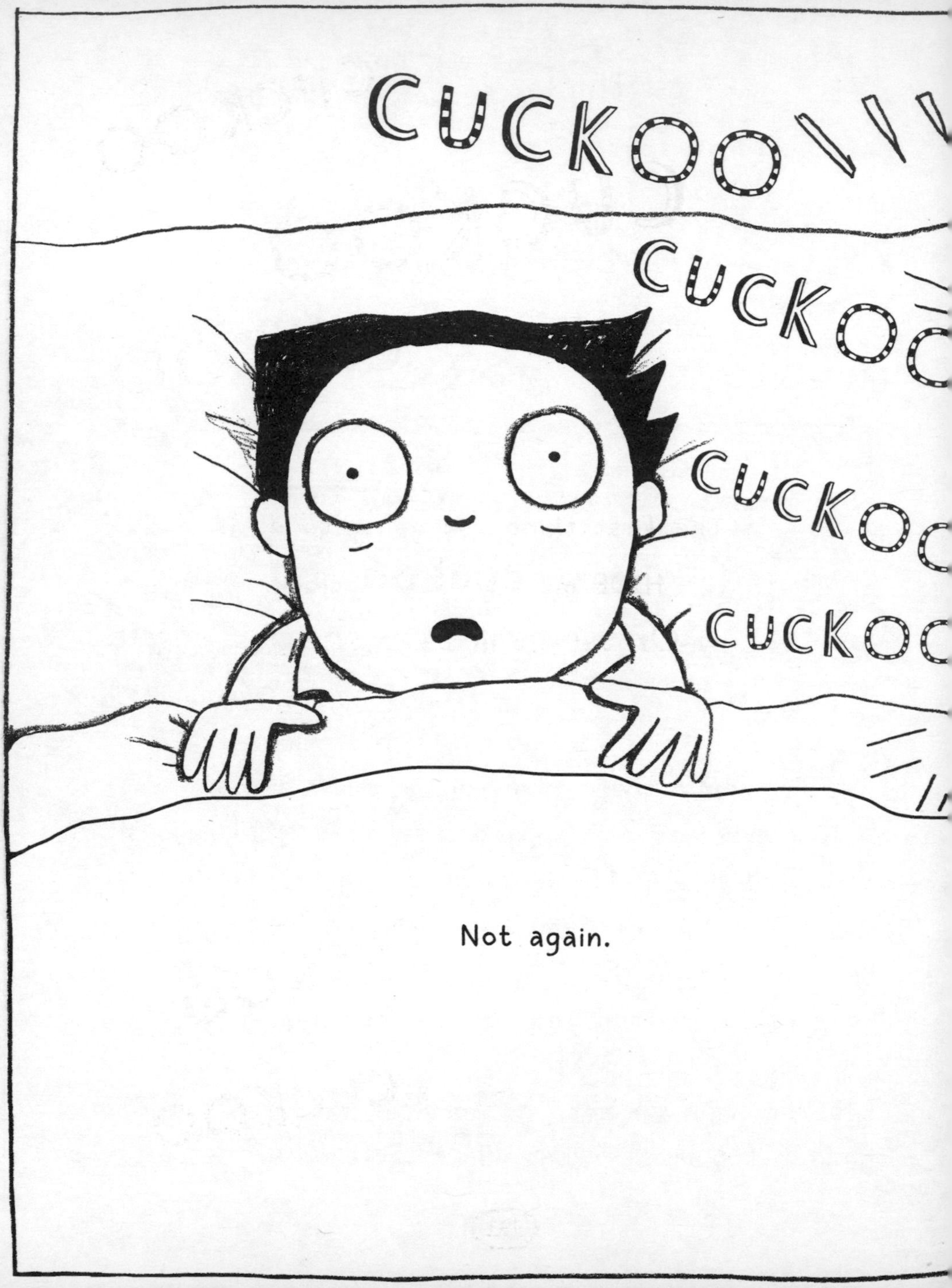
CUCKOO
CUCKOO
CUCKOO
CUCKOO
Not again.

CUCKOO

CUCKOO

CUCKOO

The first thing I'm going to do is
HIDE my cuckoo clock.
Or put it in Dad's **shed.**

CUCKOO

CUCKOO

I drag myself out of bed and go downstairs for breakfast.

Dad is busy showing Mum the FINISHED **PLASTIC CUP** posters he's done for their reunion.

 "I have no idea if they'll like it or not," Dad says.

"They look `great`. You might even get to work on their <u>NEXT</u> album if this one sells," she suggests.

"Don't count on it – I've heard the band aren't getting on too well. It could be a SHORT reunion!"

"WHAT'S that on the cover?" I ask him.

"It's a SPATULA. The songs are all about kitchen items. It's VERY **PLASTIC CUP,**" Dad explains. "They like to be different."

"Talking of people being DIFFERENT!"

(Uh-oh... I thought they'd forgotten

about my card.)

"That card, Tom. We'll never hear the end of it. Your UNCLE will bring it up all the time!"

"I can EXPLAIN!" I say.

"Not now."

Dad has to go and doesn't have time to listen.

I have to

FIND THE OTHER PART

of my note!

It's the only way to clear my name

and show I'm innocent.

(Of the card bit – not the chucking food out of the window bit... I did that.)

Derek is waiting for me and wants to know what happened last night, so I tell him.

"That's FUNNY – but annoying as well."

Then he takes me to the shop on the way to school to cheer me up (which works).

Fruit chew?

Thanks, Derek!

While we're unwrapping our sweets something VERY strange starts to happen. A couple of kids come over and ask us a question.

"Hey I recognize you TWO. Are you in a BAND called DOGZOMBIES?"

"We are – with Norman.
Why do you want to know?"

"Told you it was **THEM**," the boy says to his

friend.

Derek and I look at each other.

"That's weird. I wonder how they

know our band?" I say.

Then as we keep walking to school, someone else comes

over and TAPS me on the back.

"Are you in **DOGZOMBIES**?"

"Yes ... WHY?"

"You're **FAMOUS!**" The girl **LAUGHS**

and runs off singing **OUR** SONG.

"Is that OUR song?" Derek asks me.

(I think it IS.)

Norman comes running over to join us.

He says, "That's OUR SONG!

How does that girl know **OUR** SONG?"

It's a very GOOD question.

We haven't even PLAYED it to anyone yet. The "DOGZOMBIES Rule" video didn't exactly work out so it's ODD those kids know about the band too...

The three of us are so busy chatting about what's happened that we're ALL late for class.

Sorry.

Mr Fullerman takes two points off the chart. One for me and one for Norman.

CLASS 5F

IT'S NOT GREAT TO BE LATE.

Group 1	Group 2	Group 3	Group 4
~~50~~	50	~~50~~	~~50~~
48		~~49~~	49
~~48~~ 44		48	

You two are late.

Don't let it happen AGAIN,

he says as we go and sit down.

I sit down between Marcus and AMY and straight away Marcus starts humming a tune.

Hummmm

Hummmm

It <u>sounds</u> like "**DOGZOMBIES** Rule".

I don't say anything at first. But HE keeps on humming. Eventually I say, "THAT'S **OUR** SONG!"

"I know," Marcus tells me.

"I heard some kids singing that this morning. It's a **GOOD** SONG!" **AMY** tells me as well.

 "Really? Thanks!"

I say. But I'm <u>still</u> wondering ... HOW do they KNOW the **DOGZOMBIES** song?

(It's a **MYSTERY** - but I'm glad **AMY** likes it.)

Marcus keeps humming

loudly enough that I can hear).

Hummmm
Hummmm

"OK, Marcus – HOW do **you** know our song and WHERE did you..."

Before I can finish ⟶ Mr Fullerman interrupts.

Class 5F – today we'll be doing MATHS and some EXTRA SPELLINGS for our TEST. So we have a lot to do. But after SHAKE and WAKE! you'll all be feeling FANTASTIC.

(Not really.)

Here's my

"I'm delighted about maths and spelling" face.

← Joy

Marcus <u>won't</u> say where he heard our song.

"I have to get on with my WORK," he whispers.

"I'll tell you later..."

I try **not** to let him annoy me, but it's hard.

Learning the NEW WORDS for the

spelling test isn't EASY either.

One of the words is: **MOUSTACHE**

Sometimes drawing a picture helps me to remember
how to spell a WORD. This is the one that comes
to mind:

MOUSE
TACHE

MOUSE TACHE

Then I draw a few other ideas too.
It doesn't help with the spelling – it's just FUNNY.

Rooster
Ha!

Me
Ha!

True to
life

Mum
Ha Ha!

Time really DRAGS when you're not having FUN. So I'm looking forward to lunch. But while I'm standing in the HOT MEAL queue it happens AGAIN - a girl asks me,

"You're in DOGZOMBIES, aren't you?"

"WE'VE SEEN YOUR VIDEO!" another kid says.

"WHAT video? WE haven't done one!" I tell them. I'm CONFUSED.

Maybe there's another band called DOGZOMBIES?

"All the OLD people are singing your song on that FUNNY VIDEO website."

"That's NOT US.

It must be another band."

(What's going on?)

It's one of the dinner staff who tells me MORE about this VIDEO.

"Tom, it's SO FUNNY. There are lots of old folks and they're all AMAZING at singing and playing! And you're in it too!"

"I am?"

"They show some lovely school photos of you and pictures of your band. They're very PROUD, I think."

I take my food and go and sit down.

"I think I know what's happened," I tell Derek.

Then Marcus Meldrew finally decides to tell us where he saw the video.

"It's on the FUNNY VIDEO website. It's all gone SPIRAL..."

"You mean VIRAL," I tell him.

"Whatever – it's FUNNY."

"How did they get our song?" Derek wants to know.

"That'll be me giving a copy to Dad who gave it to Granny Mavis. What have they done with it?" I wonder out LOUD.

"I'll TELL you!" Marcus says.

(I can't shut him up now.)

He goes on about the whole video – including a bit where Granddad Bob plays the spoons.

"AND there's one old guy who plays a tiny guitar and a cup and saucer too!"

"That sounds BONKERS!" I say.

"Maybe if THIS video's doing SO well, WE don't have to make a NEW one after all?" Derek suggests.

"Loads of people have seen it, which is just what we wanted," he adds.

He's got a good point. I start to think that this could be the start of something

REALLY ⟹

I'm in a BIG HURRY to get home.

Derek and Norman come with me so we can all see what THE FOSSILS have been up to.

"This VIDEO could make our BAND REALLY POPULAR!" I say.

"We already know that old folks like it," agrees Norman (true).

As soon as we walk though the door, I see Mum waiting for me with her arms folded (which is not a good sign).

"What have you been up to NOW, Tom?" she asks. "I've had a phone call from a **NEWSPAPER** about a VIDEO and your band."

"NOTHING! It's Granny and Granddad who've been BUSY!" I tell her.

"**DOGZOMBIES** are FAMOUS!"

Norman cheers.

We all do a  high five.

"They said something about

LEAFY GREEN OLD FOLKS' HOME too.

What's THAT all about?"

Rather than spend AGES explaining

everything to Mum,

We <u>all</u> go and watch the video for ourselves.

Luckily, it's hilarious

(and not in a bad way).

Oh,
Bob!

Ha!

Ha!

Ha!

Ha!

Ha!

(for now)

School in the morning
　　And there's no one around,
It's so early
　　that you can't hear a sound,
Sitting on a bench
　　With nothing to prove,
DogZombies are here

　　And we're not gonna move,
We're in a band
　　To make you sing,
We've done a LOT
　　of practising,
We get together

　　After school,
Because we know
　　DOGZOMBIES RULE
　　　　DOGZOMBIES
　　　　　　DOGZOMBIES
　　　　　　　　DOGZOMBIES RULE (for now).

One Week Later

There's some GOOD news, some NOT-so-good news and some REALLY GOOD news.

Here's the not -so-good news – which isn't that bad.

DOGZOMBIES becoming the BIGGEST band in the WHOLE WIDE WORLD might take longer than we expected. ☹

The NEWSPAPER was only a little bit interested in our band.

It was **Teacup Tony** Ponytail

they really wanted to talk to.

Someone SPOTTED him playing the ukulele in the video and it turns out he really

was a HuGE **country-and-western** STAR.

The video was SO popular that he reunited his band and played at Granny Mavis's fundraising event for the

LEAFY GREEN OLD FOLKS' HOME.

It was a MASSIVE success and they raised LOADS of money to fix all the stuff that got broken in the POWER CUT.

Teacup Tony and the Saucers' music got played EVERYWHERE.

Loads more people bought their song **"Don't Leave Your Biscuit in the Tea Too Long"**, and it SHOT UP the charts to number ONE all over again.

Dad still did his BINGO CALLING at the event as he said he'd been practising a LOT.

Two little ducks ... 22!

And DOGZOMBIES (that's us) played our song "DOGZOMBIES Rule" as well.

Everyone joined in including Granddad Bob on the spoons and **Teacup Tony and the Saucers,** who were impressive.

Vera said the whole event was worth doing her hair for.   (Result!)

Derek's dad (Mr Fingle) is VERY happy as well.
He's found an ORIGINAL copy of their single ...

... which he says is a CLASSIC.
And might be worth some
money too. Derek told me that.

The REALLY good news is ...

I don't have to write another SORRY card to Aunty Alice and Uncle Kevin because Dad FOUND the MISSING half of the first one I made.

Yeah!

He was looking for the **newspaper** that had a "REVIEW" of the **PLASTIC CUP** reunion gig. (Apparently it didn't go too well.)

Dad found the other half of my card

SCRUNCHED up in the wastepaper bin

along with some of the paper I made the

Sorry note

MONSTERS from.

Dad said he was SORRY I got told off. I suggested that getting my OWN pet might be a REALLY nice way of saying sorry. ← Dog

(It didn't work.)

Instead when I came back from school Mum left me a note along with a few TREATS.

Which was a ➤

I ate TWO wafers and kept one for later.
Then I left THREE empty wafer wrappers
on the plate for someone else to
get fooled by.

(Delia!)

Ha! Ha!

DOGZOMBIES RULE

(for now).

Me and Derek are walking to school and we're still trying to think 🐾 😊 😊 of a new way to make DOGZOMBIES the BEST BAND EVER.

"I could ask Granddad Bob to teach me the spoons?" I suggest.

"I've got some more ideas for songs," Derek tells me, which is probably a better idea. We get to school NICE and early as neither of us can be late to class again.

IT'S NOT GREAT TO BE LATE.

Don't be late.

Surprisingly there are quite a few kids in the school grounds already.

CLASS 5F			
1	Group 2	Group 3	Group 4
	50	50	50
		45	49
4		48	

I suggest we go and sit on OUR bench, but when we start walking towards it, AMY, Florence and Brad Galloway get there before us.

"Morning, Tom and Derek," AMY says.

"Hello," we say and sit down.

"Have you forgotten then?" she adds.

I don't know WHAT AMY's talking about but I still say, "OF COURSE not."

Derek looks at me and raises his eyebrows.

"You have forgotten, haven't you?" Florence says. "It's OUR class's turn to do..."

"SHAKE and WAKE!"

Brad Galloway tells us both.

"Don't worry, we'll sit somewhere else," I tell them all.

Derek and I get up to MOVE.

I don't want to be part of another DANCE.

Even if it is AMY, Florence and Brad doing it.

"You don't have to LEAVE. You can be the first to

learn it. You're good at

SHAKE and WAKE! Tom!" AMY LAUGHs.

"Not really. I'm fine thanks," I tell her.

"You're BOTH in for a **SURPRISE!**"

Brad says.

"What kind of a **SURPRISE?**"

Derek asks.

"You'll SEE!" Florence says.

"It's REALLY ☆FUN☆!"

Brad tells us both.

"Have you got chocolate?" I ask them all.

(That's my favourite surprise.)

"No. Bad luck, Tom. You'll like it, I promise,"

AMY tries to assure me.

Then they get ready to do THEIR

SHAKE and WAKE!

Derek and I shuffle away from the FRONT as more kids start arriving.

Then the teachers turn up and Mr Keen does his SPEECH again about how GOOD this is going to be.

"I really DON'T feel like doing a crazy routine today," Derek says.

"Me neither. I'm going to do as little jumping around as possible," I tell Derek.

Then the MUSIC starts coming

out of the speakers ...

... and I change my mind.

They're playing

Here's my "I'M ACTUALLY ENJOYING DOING **SHAKE and WAKE!** AFTER ALL" face.

Watching the whole school dance to our song is actually quite FUN.

If **DOGZOMBIES** are going to TRY and be the best band in the world ...

... this is a good start.

My group came last – but I'm not that bothered after hearing what the PRIZE was...

Well done to everyone in **Group 2,** who came top of the "It's Not Great to be Late" chart!

IT'S NOT GREAT
TO BE LATE
AWARDED TO:

Cardboard clock "award"

Certificate

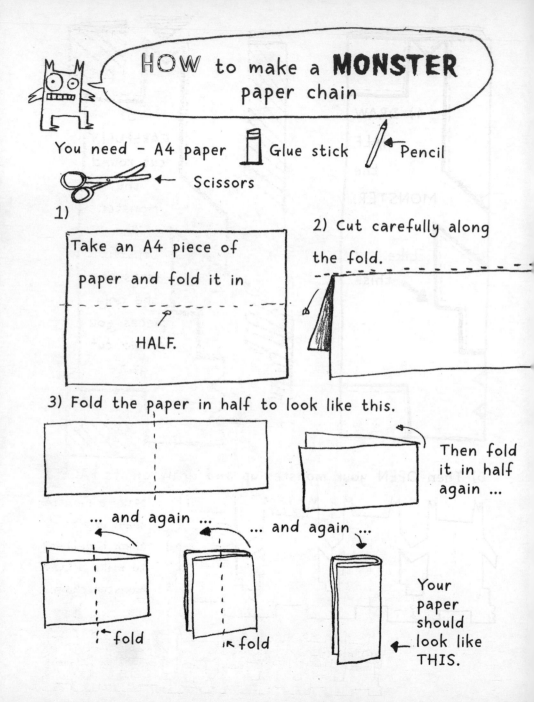

HOW to make a MONSTER paper chain

You need – A4 paper ▯ Glue stick ✏ Pencil

✂ ← Scissors

1) Take an A4 piece of paper and fold it in HALF.

2) Cut carefully along the fold.

3) Fold the paper in half to look like this.

Then fold it in half again ...

... and again ...

... and again ...

fold

fold

Your paper should look like THIS.

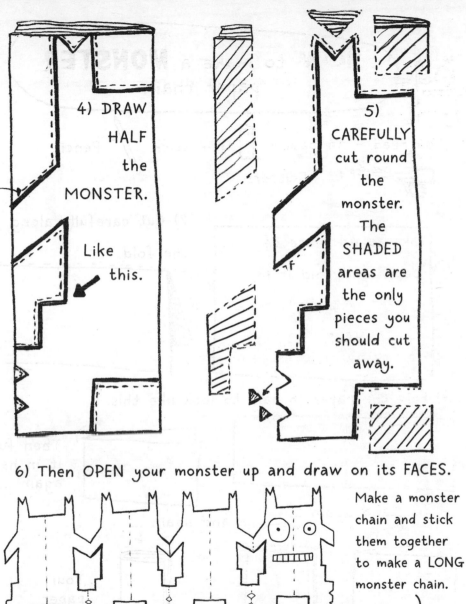

4) DRAW HALF the MONSTER.

Like this.

5) CAREFULLY cut round the monster. The SHADED areas are the only pieces you should cut away.

6) Then OPEN your monster up and draw on its FACES.

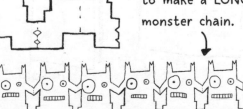

Make a monster chain and stick them together to make a LONG monster chain.

(In case you've forgotten ... it's useful.)

Follow the pictures below page.
Stretch out your fingers first (it helps).

◯ = Numbers in the circles show how many 9s.

△ = Numbers in the triangles show how many fingers to hold <u>UP</u> on the <u>left</u> side.

☐ = Numbers in the squares show how many fingers to hold <u>UP</u> on the <u>right</u> side.

Like this:

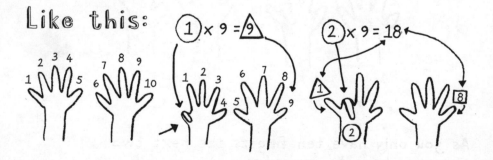

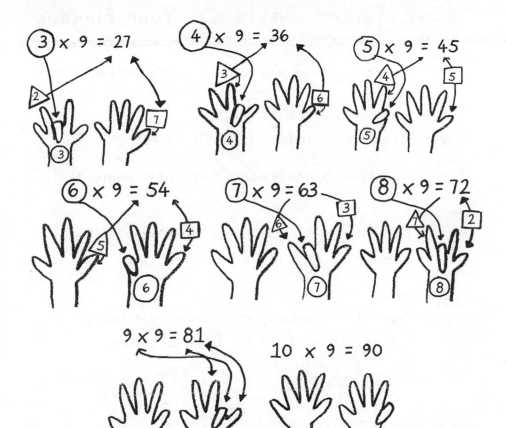

$3 \times 9 = 27$

$4 \times 9 = 36$

$5 \times 9 = 45$

$6 \times 9 = 54$

$7 \times 9 = 63$

$8 \times 9 = 72$

$9 \times 9 = 81$

$10 \times 9 = 90$

As you only have ten fingers the next two sums you have to remember.

$11 \times 9 = 99$

$12 \times 9 = 108$

www.scholastic.co.uk/tomgatesworld

Have you got ALL the TOM GATES books Yet?

When Liz was little, she loved to draw, paint and make things. Her mum used to say she was very good at making a mess (which is still true today!).

She kept drawing and went to art school, where she earned a degree in graphic design. She worked as a designer and art director in the music industry, and her freelance work has appeared on a wide variety of products.

Liz is the author-illustrator of several picture books. Tom Gates is the first series of books she has written and illustrated for older children. They have won several prestigious awards, including the Roald Dahl Funny Prize, the Waterstones Children's Book Prize, and the Blue Peter Book Award. The books have been translated into forty-one languages worldwide.

Visit her at www.LizPichon.com